My Say in the Matter

A PRO-BODILY AUTONOMY CHARITY ANTHOLOGY FOR ABORTION RIGHTS

EDITED BY EZRA ARNDT

EDITOR'S NOTE

My Say in the Matter was created in response to the overturning of Roe v. Wade in the United States Supreme Court on June 24th, 2022. The core of the anthology stems from a desire to fight against this ruling, support everyone affected by it, and express our grief and rage. As is with such work, it contains potentially triggering pieces. While I've done my best to list everything I could find here, there may be thematically triggering material in this book as well not mentioned below. The content notice goes as follows: *body horror, transphobia, descriptions of blood, choking, murder, sexism, fertility, childbirth, family expectations, boundary setting, a mention of knives, themes of anger and survivorship, suicide, suggested sexual assault, the dehumanization of people, intimate partner violence, alluded to rape, non-consensual impregnation (there's no intercourse), religious trauma, generational trauma, termination, dubious consent/non-consent, cursing, death, grave-robbing, implied past abuse, and semi-erotic content.*

For anyone with or who has had a uterus affected by this bullshit ruling. Let's show them what we're made of.

RESURRECTION

Alanna Felton

Justyna wiped her paintbrush on the hem of her robes, adding to the assortment of streaks and splotches already staining the gray fabric. She knew Mother Lizaveta would scold her for the careless gesture if the Abbess were here. On her rare visits to Justyna's cell, Lizaveta always reprimanded Justyna for giving the Sisters in the laundry additional work, never mind that Justyna hadn't washed her robes in weeks.

She dipped her paintbrush in safflower oil to cleanse it, setting it to dry on the windowsill next to a row of candles burned down to stubs and trailing dried rivers of wax down the wall. Justyna took a step back to inspect her work in the candles' dim amber glow: oil paint on a wooden rectangle the size of Justyna's torso depicting a slender girl with gaping black hollows in the place where her eyes should have been, weeping bloody tears.

Saint Danika the All-Seeing: Gifted with prophecy. Eyes gouged out by Prince Volos for opposing his heretical reign. Patron of the blind and the precocious.

Something—not pleasure or satisfaction, those feelings had long since become foreign, but some interruption in the fog of numbness which Justyna spent her days lost in—stirred in her chest. The icon was one of her best yet; Justyna had finally managed the trick of blending and layering pigments to create the illusion of light and shadow. Danika's fair skin shone as if lit from within, the drops of blood sliding down her cheeks gleamed like rubies. The Saint's features contorted in an expression that was equal parts agony and enlightenment, her lips parted in a silent plea that was at once a scream and a prayer.

In her two months spent behind the red walls of the Convent of the Lake, Justyna had only set foot in the cathedral a handful of times, always at the behest of Mother Lizaveta. Most days she ignored the ringing of the bells that called the Sisters to worship, devoting all her time to painting.

Justyna usually rose before the sun and did not stumble into bed until longer after it had set. Her days bled into one another much like the reds and tans and greens and golds of her pallet, passing in a fervor of sketches and brushstrokes. Pressing charcoal into sheets of parchment until they tore. Layering swathes of gleaming pigment on top of wooden boards until the paint took on its own texture and dimension. Drawing and then painting women and girls, over and over again, their heads wreathed in golden light, their figures bloody and broken. All Saints. All martyrs. All dead.

The air in Justyna's cell was thick with the scent of paint. On the rare occasions when nuns or other novitiates visited to bring her meals or fresh supplies, their eyes watered and they doubled over coughing from the strength of the fumes. Justyna had long since become inured to the odor of linseed; she breathed it in, tasted it on her tongue every second of every day. It seeped into her clothes and her bedsheets, into the walls of her cell, until she did not remember that the world had ever smelled otherwise.

She worked without pause and often completed as many as three paintings in one day. Whenever she finished an icon, Justyna would mount it to the wall using nails and twine. It was not long before they crowded the stone walls of her cell, often overlapping.

Her paintings were unlike the portraits of saints decorating the icon screen in the cathedral. Those illustrations were as flat as the wood they were painted on, lacking depth or value. They faced forward in identical poses, gazing straight ahead through empty inkblot eyes, hands clasped in prayer. The men wore elaborate robes and armor, the women beautiful gowns. They were all healthy and hale, regardless of how they had achieved sainthood. Justyna could not stand to sit through services in the cathedral beneath those perfect beings' dispassionate gazes. The icons looking down upon her as she worked were depicted at the moments of their martyrdoms, their expressions fearful, furious, shocked—anything but still and serene. They were bleeding out, burning up, drowning, dismembered.

Icon Number One: A curvaceous redhead with wide green eyes and full lips, clothes torn, hands clutching a dagger buried in her chest.

Saint Vesna the Comely: Gifted with beauty. Killed herself rather than be ravished by Prince Iakov. Patron of loyal daughters and unwed women.

Icon Number Four: A near-unrecognizable figure whose skin was blackened and charred, the white gleam of bone visible in some places.

Saint Filipa the Kind: Gifted with communion with all beasts. Burned at the stake by northern barbarians. Patron of hunters and horsemen.

Icon Number Thirteen: An armored form bristling with the feathered shafts of arrows, her neck a bloodied stump, holding her head on a platter before her.

Saint Tamarah the Brave: Gifted with strength. Beheaded in battle by Prince Radomil after his men shot her full of arrows. Patron of soldiers slain in battle.

A copy of The Book of Saints lay discarded in one corner of her cell. Justyna had long since rendered it unnecessary, memorizing each of the martyred lady Saints' tales. She recited them to herself sometimes, muttering as she painted until the words took on a rhythm of their own, a litany that she offered up to the Gods.

The lady Saints were Justyna's constant companions, often the only other faces she saw for days on end. Their somber visages watched over her as she worked, the candlelight tossing shadows across their faces that gave their static expressions the appearance of movement. Sometimes Justyna even imagined she'd glimpsed a curl from a set of downturned lips or a blink from a pair of wide-open eyes, there and gone in the span of a single breath.

The whole convent was aflutter with rumors about the new novitiate who rarely attended service, did not complete any chores, and passed all her days holed up in her room, her only regular communications with the other Sisters messages requesting fresh paints and wood panels.

"It isn't fair!" Novice Alma said one morning over breakfast. "The Sisters let her do whatever she wants."

Novice Sashura rolled her eyes. "Her father is richer than all the Gods in Heaven and Devils in Hell combined. No one's going to try bossing Justyna after what he paid the convent to take her off his hands."

"It's blatant favoritism. Besides," Alma's pout shifted into a grin that was all teeth and meanness, "Justyna hardly belongs in a convent. I've heard rumors about her and Prince Andrei's son..."

"Ahem." Sister Yesfir glared at the two novitiates. "I believe you both have better things to do than linger and gossip."

"Yes, Sister Yesfir." Alma and Sashura both flushed and scattered beneath Yesfir's gaze.

That night, when Yesfir lay down to sleep, her thoughts kept circling back to Alma's words, to her memories of the day that Justyna joined the convent.

The girl arrived clad in a silk gown and dripping with jewels, her garb more suited to a nobleman's halls than a life of piety. Yesfir recalled how pale Justyna had been, slouching beneath the weight of her fine clothes. The twin crescents beneath the girl's eyes, so dark they could have been bruises, and the peeling skin of her bottom lip, as if she had been worrying it with her teeth.

Yesfir was tasked with seeing Justyna settled while Mother Lizaveta conferred with the girl's father, a great pillar of a man dressed in silks and brocades even more luxurious than his daughter's.

Justyna trailed after Yesfir like a leashed pet, mute save the occasional "Yes, Sister" or "No, Sister."

Doubtless, Justyna's cell was plainer than any quarters the girl was used to, but she did not complain, just took in the small room—stone walls, a desk and chair, a single pallet with a set of robes folded on top of it—with a level gaze.

Yesfir was about to take her leave when Justyna spoke.

"Can you bring me painting supplies?" The girl's voice was hesitant, scarcely above a whisper. "I wish to make icons."

Sunlight poured through the window behind Justyna, silhouetting her slight form. She could almost be an icon herself, some virgin martyr crowned with a golden halo, but for her eyes. A set of twin tourmaline chips, so dark that irises and pupils bled together, creating the impression of shadowed pits. Something stirred in their dark depths, something *furious* which Yesfir could not put words to but which filled her with a dim sense of dread all the same.

"I will talk to Mother Lizaveta." Yesfir said, though she already knew the answer. She had recognized what kind of man Justyna's father was from the first—golden rings lining his fingers, an imperious set to his chin. She doubted they could afford to deny this girl anything.

As Yesfir tossed and turned in bed, she wondered, not for the first time, what Justyna was hiding. The girl had gotten herself into some kind of trouble, that much was obvious. Wealthy families did not send their daughters to convents except as a last resort.

I've heard rumors about her and Prince Andrei's son...

Alma and Sashura were silly girls, prone to exaggeration. And yet...Yesfir thought once again of Justyna's luxurious clothes, of the harried, secretive look on her father's face. Before she drifted off to sleep, Yesfir resolved to speak to Mother Lizaveta about the matter the next day.

But when Yesfir rose at dawn there were chores to be done and prayers to be said, leaving no room for thoughts of Justyna. The nun did not speak to Lizaveta that day, or the next, or the day after that. She forgot all about Alma and Sashura's whisperings, until the morning, nearly a month later, when a handsome young man appeared at the convent gates. He wore a sleek fur cloak over his tunic and was accompanied by two guards. Both of the men had swords on their belts and loomed over Yesfir, broad-shouldered and thick-necked, violence written in the sets of their mouths.

"I've come for Justyna," the young man said, his smile the lazy, self-assured grin of a person used to getting his way. Even from a distance, Yesfir could smell the oil used to slick back his hair and beard, an overwhelming aroma of cedar and bergamot that made her nostrils burn.

"Novice Justyna is busy with her initiation." Yesfir said, straightening her shoulders and drawing herself up to her full height. "She cannot see visitors."

The young man's smile fell away so suddenly that it was as if the expression had never been there to begin with. "Ahem." He adjusted the collar of his tunic, drawing attention to a heavy gold ring encircling his right thumb. The ring was engraved with the image of a snake curled around a battle axe—Prince Andrei's seal.

Yesfir blanched and dropped into a bow. "I did not know... forgive me, Sir—"

"Stepan." He made a dismissive gesture. "And it's quite alright. Just take me to Justyna."

Yesfir wanted to bolt the gate fast, hasten to Justyna's cell and warn the poor girl to run, hide. But who was Yesfir to defy a Prince's son? She would not be responsible for bringing Andrei's wrath down upon her Sisters.

Stomach sinking, Yesfir stood aside and gestured for Stepan and his men to enter. The four of them walked through the courtyard without conversation; their steps reverberating with all din of church bells.

"May I... may I ask what you want with Novice Justyna?" Yesfir at last found the courage to say.

"Don't you know?" Stepan's lips parted into a grin that put Justyna in mind of a wolf contemplating his prey, his incisors gleaming. "Justyna will never join the convent. She is to be my bride."

I've heard rumors about her and Prince Andrei's son...

Yesfir had suspected, had known, really, but the words still landed like a blow. If what Sashura had implied in her whisperings, what Stepan was currently implying in his every glance and gesture, was true, then Justyna *would* never join the Sisters. The novitiate was Stepan's by right.

When they reached the door to Justyna's cell, Stepan gestured for the four of them to halt. "Thank you for guiding us Sister, but I'd prefer to speak privately with my intended." He inclined his head with reverence, but there was mockery in the curl of his lips and the hard glint of his eyes. His guards loomed over Yesfir; scarred knuckles clenching the hilts of their weapons.

And so Yesfir left, Gods help her. She told herself that there was nothing she could do for Justyna, that the girl had brought this upon herself. The Convent of the Lake had no business trying to protect a girl who could not even protect her own virtue.

Justyna knelt on the floor of her cell, unaware of all that had just transpired, gazing up at her Saints. She had completed her final icon that morning—a dark-haired girl drenched in water and bound in chains, foam-capped waves rising to consume her.

Saint Marzena the Silver-Tongued: Gifted with wisdom. Clapped in irons and drowned by benighted villagers. Patron of scholars, scribes, and poets.

Like her sister Saints, Marzena was cut down early in life by men who did not understand her gifts. Not for the first time, Justyna wondered what it was like to be blessed in that way, to at least know that one's mortal anguish would be rewarded with transcendent martyrdom in death.

Someone entered her cell without knocking, flinging her door open with such force that it slammed into the wall. The scent of cedar and bergamot drifted into the room, warring with paint fumes for dominance.

Justyna leaped to her feet at the sound, heart pounding. She knew, without setting eyes on the interloper, who it was.

"Hello, Justyna," Stepan's tone was light, but Justyna remembered how suddenly his benevolence could curdle into cruelty. "Did you really think you could hide from me?"

Justyna did not turn around. She remained rooted to the spot, eyes fixed upon the maimed and mutilated forms of women who had been singled out for greatness by the Gods and made to suffer for it. She tried to slow her racing pulse, her ragged breathing, to little avail. When she opened her mouth to speak, the words caught in her throat; she struggled without success to push them off her tongue.

"Well?" Stepan snapped. He had always hated being ignored. The nobleman's footsteps sounded thudded against the stone floor and then he was grabbing Justyna by the shoulders, pulling her around to face him. His large fingers gripped her chin with bruising strength as his dark eyes bored into hers. "Look at me!"

Justyna still could not speak, not even to apologize, not even to beg Stepan to just leave her be. She just stared back at him, quaking like an animal caught in a snare.

Almost as quickly as it had appeared, Stepan's anger vanished like smoke rising, the mask of geniality falling back into place. "Your paintings are quite lovely, if morbid," he said, smirking. His tone was silken with satisfaction, secure in the knowledge that Justyna still feared him, that he was still in control. "I never took you to be a pious type. Does this have anything to do with how we met?"

The room around Justyna fell away and she was standing in a crowded banquet hall on a cold night nearly two months ago, her hair braided with snowdrop blossoms to celebrate the Festival of Saint Filipa. Prince Andrei's son, the most handsome man Justyna had ever seen, was making eyes at her from across the room. She was blushing as her friends teased her about it, meeting Stepan's unabashed gaze with shy, fleeting glances. She was curtsying as Stepan approached, other guests parting like a sea before him. She was nodding mutely as the Prince asked her to dance, unable to believe her luck. She was laughing at Stepan's remarks while her heart fluttered at the sensation of his hand clutching her waist. She was politely trying to extricate herself from Stepan's grasp after the dance ended, her excitement twisting into panic as he pulled her closer instead, his hands sliding lower. She was following along as Stepan pulled her into a dark room, ignoring her gentle protests. She was not daring to say no, even when she desperately wanted to. Never daring to say no...

The odor and taste of linseed, blended with the intrusive aroma of Stepan's perfume, cut through the fog of Justyna's memories. Her gaze flickered to the icons papering the walls all around her. She was no Saint. The Gods had not blessed her and she could not leave the prison of her corrupted flesh behind, no matter how she despised it at times. But she knew these women—their stories, their pain, their shame, their anger—as well as she knew herself.

She would not be frightened of this man. She would not hate herself or her body because of him. Not anymore.

Justyna took a deep breath, met Stepan's glare. "Let me go."

Stepan dug his fingers deeper into Justyna's skin, pulling her forward by the jaw so that her face was just a breath away from his. Justyna cried out. "What. Did you just say. To me." He spoke through gritted teeth, the words less a question than a command.

Justyna's fear ebbed away like the tide receding, leaving a calm, cold kind of fury in its place. The worst had already happened; she had already lost her virtue, her status, her family, her home. What would happen if she let go of all the shame and guilt and self-loathing she had been made to feel? What could she become?

Stepan had sought to make a martyr of her, but he made a grave mistake when he failed to finish the job and left her alive.

The nobleman saw Justyna's expression change and was so startled that he took a step back, releasing his hold on her. His eyes widened and his Adam's apple bobbed up and down, his hands raised in reflexive defense.

Good. It was his turn to know fear.

Something unfurled inside Justyna, something jagged and vicious. The girl she had been two months ago would have cowered before it. Now, she welcomed it with open arms. A grin pulled at her lips.

"Guards!" Stepan shouted, and two armed men burst into the room.

Justyna paid them no mind. She prayed, not to the distant Gods that had never protected her. She prayed to her Saints, to the women who knew what it was to have their bodies, their youth, their potential stolen. Stolen, but not lost. She prayed, and her Saints listened. Her Saints awoke.

Fabric rustled, armor clinked, bone scraped as the paintings mounted on Justyna's walls came to life. The lady Saints emerged from their icons, not as figures rendered in oil brushstrokes, but as fully formed beings of flesh, trailing blood and ash in their wake. A horde of grotesqueries glowing golden with divine light.

Saint Danika, her steps certain despite her blindness. Saint Vesna, pulling the dagger from her breast and brandishing it before her. Saint Filipa, charred flesh falling from her bones. Saint Tamarah, her head in one hand and a sword in the other. Saint Marzena, shivering and blue-lipped.

All of them and almost two dozen more women and girls, some walking, some shuffling, some crawling forward on broken and severed and mangled limbs, their collective focus bearing down on Stepan and his men. They crowded the cell, standing shoulder-to-shoulder, packing the space, carrying the smoky, sickly-sweet scent of burnt skin, the damp musk of river water, the metallic odor of blood.

The Saints clawed, beat, kicked, gouged, slashed, hacked without relent. They did not, could not speak, their expressions frozen as Justyna had painted them, but the women's dead eyes gleamed with a kind of exaltation as they returned the violence men had dealt them tenfold.

Stepan and his men's screams filled Justyna's cell, a strange hymnal for her strange shrine. The guards lashed out with their swords to no avail. There was no killing women who were already dead.

Justyna simply stood there, ignoring Stepan's increasingly unintelligible pleas. She and her Saints were the monsters that men had made of them, and they would not be merciful. Vesna turned and handed Justyna her dagger, now slick with blood.

Justyna smiled, the first true smile to grace her features in months. She gazed down at what was left of Stepan and raised the blade. "I told you to let me go."

THE GIRL IN THE MAGIC TRICK

STEPHANIE PARENT

I dreamt of the ropes kissing my wrists
   the way some girls dream of Prince Charming's
lips
   others of white dresses, or white horses
   or their bodies on silver screens, voices over
radio waves

ascending beyond this world—

My deepest desires were for constriction
thick ropes and silky sashes
alternated the starring roles
confining my limbs, sealing my lips
darkening my vision as my insides
lit up.

I grew older and feared to speak
my dreams aloud. Whenever I was paired
with another, my desires stayed
silent—my gag, invisible. My limbs
became a burden. In my mind, my body
turned heavy, hideous, and cold.

Ashamed, I fled to solitude,
private visions of
railroad tracks—

Till he saw me, snuck up from behind
a silent train derailing me
knocking me flat
bending my body backward, strapping
me into unnatural
shapes that felt right,
so right that

though I could not move,
I flew.

Blindfolded, I did not foresee
the wreckage; I opened my eyes
too late.

There was only one thing left to do:
I found scissors and

cut through knotted twine, like
knife through gristle

opened my eyes to the
real world

and sawed my own
way out.

THE HERB IN THE WOOD

MORGAN DAIMLER

Into the Wood I

"My lady, you cannot mean to do this," Morag said, clutching Elayne's heavy green cloak in her hands.

"It's my wood, my father gave it to me," Elayne said, pulling the cloak from her maid's nervous hands. "It's only right I get some use from it. And I'm tired of always riding by the riverside, I want something new today."

"Your father is the earl of Selkirk," Morag said, "you can ride wherever you please."

Elayne frowned but shook her head, "You know he prefers I not ride too far without an escort. There are only a few places he approves of for me to go alone and I'm bored of all of them."

"But my lady," Morag protested, her eyes darting around the empty bedroom as if she was worried they would be overheard. "Everyone says that Chartre Woods is haunted by an elf-man who takes a toll of maidens who pass by. They say he robs girls of their gold, or any green they wear, or...or...*seduces* them."

"I'm not afraid of spirits," Elayne said, wrapping the cloak around her shoulders and pulling her brown hair free with one hand. "And I won't submit to superstition. It's the 17th century, people should know better than to believe in such things."

In truth, she was as afraid of the supernatural as anyone else, but she didn't want to seem that way, especially to Morag who she knew would quickly tell all the other girls in the keep. Elayne liked her maid well enough, but the younger woman was flighty and prone to fancy and she couldn't keep her mouth closed for anything. It wasn't exactly the best quality in a maid, but for Elayne, who was alone too often, the other woman's chatter about the goings-on at the keep provided entertainment and a sense of belonging that was comforting. "If I want to go to the Wood then I shall and no elf will stop me."

Morag's only reply was to cross herself and mutter a prayer, which Elayne ignored. She pulled the cloak tight and brushed by the maid, striding purposefully down the hallway, through the keep towards the stables. She knew that everyone was afraid of the Wood and she suspected that was part of why her father had gifted it to her – a place that was haunted and useless except as a refuge for wild deer; a gift that showed his generosity without risking any of his courtiers or farmers complaining he'd taken usable land away from them. Well, she'd get some use out of it despite all the stories; she was wearing a gold ring and a green cloak and if the elf did exist in the Wood he could have his pick of either, although she rather thought she'd be coming home exactly as she'd left.

The stablehand had already saddled Elayne's sturdy little horse so she swung into the saddle and headed off, trotting north towards Chartre Wood instead of taking her usual route east along the river. The change of scenery was nice, the path slowly wending along, and she found herself relaxing, enjoying the late August day despite the overcast sky. The trees were just starting to lose their leaves, the ground strewn with orange, yellow, and red, her horse's hooves making a soft sound as they traveled along. The way through the Wood was overgrown but not impassable, and she followed it beneath the early autumn trees as it wound on until she came to a small clearing. At the back of the clearing was what looked like an old well, badly overgrown with wild roses.

Elayne's breath caught at the sight of the flowers, still blooming despite the lateness of the season, and she slid off her mount. Quickly tying her reins to a nearby oak, she walked across the open space and leaned towards the riot of blooms, inhaling deeply. The flower petals were dark red, a sharp contrast to the roses' brighter green leaves and yellow thorns; they were the most beautiful roses she'd ever seen, so vivid among the shadowed trees they seemed unreal. Without thinking she reached out and picked one, the stem snapping under her fingers. A thorn pricked her skin, a single drop of blood sliding down and dropping into the flowers below, red on red.

"Who are you to dare break even a twig in this Wood?"

Elayne startled at the voice and spun away from the roses and well, turning to find a man and horse behind her. The hair on her arms rose at the uncanniness of their silent arrival, and she stepped further back unable to hide her unease.

The stranger stood near the edge of the clearing, staring curiously at her. He was the most handsome person Elayne had ever seen, almost unbelievably so, his dark hair falling in waves past his shoulders,

his eyes a piercing green that shone in his pale face
which looked like the work of a master sculptor.
His clothing was as fine as the rest of him, silk
and leather, highlighting his lean muscular form,
and he carried himself with an ease and confidence
that fit his appearance. At first, Elayne judged him
to be around her own age, perhaps in his early
twenties, but the longer she looked the less certain
she was. There was something old in his eyes, a
hardness that lingered behind the noble facade and
belied the youthfulness of everything else. At his
side stood a horse who was better than any in her
father's possession: a dappled grey with silver bells
woven into his mane.

Elayne knew she hadn't heard any bells—or
anything else—and again the unnaturalness of it
struck her. On the other edge of the clearing, her
little horse snorted nervously, pulling away from
the newcomers so that the reins that tied her to the
tree grew taut.

Summoning all her courage she answered
his question, "I am Elayne, daughter of Lord
Donnchadh, and this is my Wood."

"Yours?" The stranger laughed lightly, as if she'd
said something very funny.

"Yes, mine," Elayne said, squaring her shoulders.
"My father gave it to me."

"Your father is bold to give what belongs to
us," he said, still laughing. His eyes were grim,
though, and it sent a shiver through her to see.
There was danger here, and she suddenly regretted

ignoring Morag's warning and not having any iron on her. Iron was supposed to ward off the Good Neighbors.

"It belongs to me," she insisted, her voice weaker than before as she began to realize how much trouble she was in.

"And you are bold to claim what belongs to us," he said, smirking at her in open condescension.

"I don't even know who you are," she said, although she was very much afraid she did.

He tsked slightly. "I'm Tam, the guardian of this well for the People of the Hills who claim this place as *ours*. Surely you've heard the stories. Surely you know that you are trespassing and that all who trespass here owe me a toll."

She swallowed loudly, wilting under the weight of his words. "I have a gold ring and this green cloak—"

"Oh, I think I have enough of rings and cloaks," he said, his handsome face shining brighter as if lit from within. "I think I know exactly what toll I'll have from you."

Elayne shook her head slowly, dazzled by his beauty but also afraid. "I don't want to."

"Of course you do," he said, reasonable and calm, crossing the space between them. "They always do. And I promise, my pretty Elayne, that you'll enjoy yourself and say yes soon enough. No one ever refuses me for long."

His voice was like honey and his presence was like wine, sweet and intoxicating. Elayne felt her thoughts clouding as he pulled her close and started kissing her, her resolve crumbling. She felt like she was in a dream that she couldn't wake from, her world narrowed down to his hands and lips and body and the growing heat between them. It was hard to think, hard to remember why she'd ever wanted anything but to be in his arms.

"Tell me that you want me," he purred.

Dazzled and dizzy she nodded, her eyes closing as she sagged into his arms, unable to resist the enchantment he'd woven.

The Courtyard

Two months after her visit to the Wood, Elayne knew she'd come away that day with more than just grass stains on her dress, but she had no idea what she was going to do. She felt desperation closing in with each passing day. Her father had always been lenient with her, spoiled her even, but he'd never permit her to bear a bastard, it would be too scandalous. He'd been willing to let her choose a husband herself when she found someone that suited her, but this would force his hand. He'd insist she marry as quickly as possible, someone he chose who'd be willing to accept the situation she was in, and she knew those possibilities would be very limited. Of course, she could be honest about what had happened, but while there were some who would believe her if she told the truth they'd also mock her arrogance in daring to go to Chartre Wood despite all the warnings.

She wasn't sure which was worse, the thought of marrying someone her father chose or being laughed at forever as the woman who dared the elfin well and came away with a child from it.

"Are you unwell my lady?" Morag asked as she helped Elayne dress. The maid's voice was worried but Elayne couldn't help the paranoid assumption that the other woman knew about her predicament. And once Morag knew she'd spread the news to everyone. Elayne winced, smoothing her skirt.

"I'm overtired," she said, hoping that sounded believable. It should since she found sleep elusive these days. "I haven't been sleeping well."

"Are you dreaming of the Wood, my lady?" Morag asked, tightening the ties at Elayne's back.

Elayne felt all the blood draining from her face at the thought, and whispered, "Yes."

It was the truth, albeit a painful one. She'd been haunted by dreams – or nightmares, she wasn't entirely certain which – since that day. She told no one what had happened after she'd returned, not even Morag who had questioned her for days about it. Even now she wouldn't speak of it.

"I know it's not my place, my lady," Morag said, finishing with the dress and moving to fetch Elayne's shoes. "But I know a man who's knowledgeable about the Good Neighbours. If it's some enchantment that's seized you he could set you right."

Elayne doubted that very much, but she forced a smile. "That's kind of you to offer, but I'm not under any enchantment. If he has any remedies for sleep, that I could use."

Morag helped Elayne slip her shoes on then stood, brushing dust from her dress, "I don't think he has any but I do know a woman, a cunning woman, a few villages over who may be able to help you with that...or other things."

"That's alright," Elayne said, waving her off and ignoring the implication. She wasn't quite desperate enough yet to risk that sort of help, not when it would mean the whole keep knowing about her predicament. She just couldn't trust Morag not to spread the tale. "I'm sure it will sort itself out."

Morag looked as if she wanted to say something else, making Elayne feel even more paranoid, but she closed her mouth and just nodded. Trying to ignore the maid's staring and her own queasy stomach, Elayne pushed past her and out the door, moving down the hallways toward the main courtyard. It was a sunny day and the young ladies of the keep were going to play a game of ball. Elayne didn't want to, but it would look suspicious if she didn't show, especially as she'd missed the sewing circle the day before.

She emerged into the sunlight of the courtyard and all conversation stopped.

She knew then, whether it was Morag guessing and talking or too many people noticing things Elayne couldn't hide, that the rumors had started. She fought the urge to turn and run back to her rooms, forcing herself to continue on towards the group of women across the yard instead.

Her father and several of his men were standing nearby and she had no choice but to walk past them. As she did one of her father's knights, an older man named Hugh, caught her eye and grinned. He was a cruel man who had always delighted in teasing Elayne until she cried and then claiming she was too sensitive.

"Forgive me if I speak out of turn my lord," Hugh said loudly, still smirking at Elayne, "but everyone is saying that your daughter goes with child. We've been waiting for you to announce her marriage."

The words rang through the silent space and every head turned towards her, people openly staring now. She would've ignored him and kept going but her father stopped her.

"Is this true, Elayne?" Her father's voice was resigned as if he already knew the answer. She wondered why he hadn't spoken to her privately if he'd heard the rumors.

She lifted her chin, refusing to be shamed before the crowd. "I have done nothing wrong, father."

He sighed, looking older than his years. "Are you pregnant? Tell me plainly if you are and name the father, or else if you won't name him I will find you a good man and have you wed before the week is out. You are my only child and heir to my lands, you won't be refused."

She struggled not to wince at the way he said it, knowing the man he'd find would undoubtedly be his own age at best and probably already having buried at least three wives—who else wouldn't care that her child wasn't his but a man with a dozen heirs already? Her father had always been kind to her, spoiled her people said, and he'd been content to let her choose her own way in her own time, but she knew this situation would force his hand. She kept her chin up when she spoke. "If I go with child, father, then there's no mortal man that's responsible for it, only an elfin knight. And I wouldn't marry any man but that one, and I wouldn't marry him for anything."

Several people laughed at her words, thinking that she was trying to make a joke of it, but her father's eyes were serious. "If the rumors are false then I won't force you into a marriage. But if there is truth in them then you must do what is best for yourself and this family. The truth will out, Elayne, either way."

"I swear to you, father, there is no man in this keep or these lands or all of mortal earth who could claim to have done anything with me that could justify these rumors," she said, far more boldly than she felt. It was the truth but she knew that she had precious little time now to solve the problem she'd found herself in.

Her father smiled and she watched the tension flow from him because he knew she wouldn't lie and certainly wouldn't swear to a lie. He reached out and absently patted her arm before turning back to the men. "Well enough of that nonsense, then. I'll hear no more against my daughter from any of you. Let's get to the stables and see if our luck in the hunt is as good as this fine weather."

She breathed a soft sigh of relief, but she knew this was only the beginning and that soon enough there would be no denying or diverting from the truth. As she went on the rest of the women turned away, busying themselves with setting up the game and studiously avoiding looking at her.

"Elayne."

She turned at the sound of her name, searching until she noticed Katherine standing near the wall. They had been friends when they were younger before Katherine's family married her off and her time was taken up with her children. Curious, Elayne moved over to where the other woman was standing with her youngest child in her arms. "Hello, Katherine."

Katherine adjusted the baby in her arms, looking anxiously around to be sure the other women had all dispersed. When she spoke she didn't look at Elayne. "There's an herb that grows in Chartre Wood, a bitter herb, that can help you."

"Help me? Help me how?" Elayne asked, hope surging in her chest.

"If you prepare it a certain way it will bring on your menstruation," Katherine said, her voice low, her eyes still wandering around the courtyard. "But you must use it soon. It only works up to a certain point."

"Tell me," Elayne said.

Into the Wood II

She hoped that she wouldn't run into him again since she wasn't going back near that accursed well. Her feelings about him were a tangle of things, some unpleasant and some joyous so that she couldn't sort any of it out. She didn't want to see him because she was afraid that as with the first time, she'd find herself powerless against him. His presence was overwhelming, and she never wanted to feel that helpless again. So she followed Katherine's directions, leaving the shadowed path before the well where a lightning-struck oak stood just off the path. She searched until she found the plant that her friend had described, growing in a thick cluster that formed its own small grove among the rocks near an old stone wall. The plants were nearly as wide as they were tall, the leaves thin-lobed and blueish-green, nearly silver, exactly as Katherine had said they would be. With an almost dizzying sense of relief, she quickly started harvesting as much as she could.

He appeared as he had before, without any sound or warning, a silent shadow slipping from the cover of the trees. "Why are you pulling the bitter herb, Elayne? Why do you not want the child we've made between us?"

Elayne froze at his voice, the plants she'd collected clutched in her fist. Turning, she found him standing several feet away, his eyes on her sharp and measuring. He was still breathtakingly beautiful, too much to be real, and despite herself she stopped and admired him, wishing that he was only a dream and not a cold reality. He closed the distance between them and she shuddered as his hand slipped over her arm, that insidious desire warring with repulsion. Steeling herself, she said, "I can't go through this pregnancy alone and I won't marry any of the men my father would have me choose from."

"There is an easy solution to that," he said, smiling gently at her although the light of it never reached his eyes. "I was a mortal man once before the Fairy Queen stole me away to guard her well. You can win me back to mortal life and I can marry you."

She turned to face him, his hand sliding from her arm, frowning and looking for the trap behind his words. "How would that work?"

His smile grew, dark and satisfied as if he was already assured of her cooperation. "The Fairy Court rides tonight and you can win my freedom if you are brave enough – and I don't doubt you are. Go at midnight to the crossroads in the Wood and bring holy water with you, blessed in a Christian church. What kind doesn't matter. Use it to make a circle around yourself and you'll be hidden from our eyes."

"You can't see me if I use holy water?" Elayne asked, surprised that such a simple thing would be so effective.

He frowned at the interruption. "Only if you use it properly. But yes, if you do as I say with it you will be hidden from the elfin Host."

He paused, watching her, and she hastily nodded. Satisfied, he went on, "When you see the cavalcade pass by, look for me on the white horse near the queen's side. I'm given the honor of that place because I was once a mortal man and the queen favors me."

"You were human once?" Elayne cut in again, unable to stop herself. She hadn't imagined he could ever have been human.

He looked annoyed for an instant then quickly smoothed his expression over into something more pleasant. "Yes, I was born as human as you. But I was stolen away by the Queen of Elfland. Just think of what an amazing thing you will do by rescuing me and returning me to mortal life."

Elayne nodded slowly, her mind spinning at what she'd just been told.

He was going on eagerly now. "Pull me down and hold me tight. She will turn me in your arms to fearsome things, to a wolf, and lion, and bear, and snake, and a burning brand, and flame. But as I am the father of your child I will do you no harm. Hold me tight and then she will relent and turn me to a naked man. You have only to cover me with your cloak then and I will be free. And then we can wed and you will have the finest husband in this whole land."

Elayne's mind raced as she thought of everything he'd said and of why he took the toll at the well that he did. "And if I wasn't pregnant? Could I still rescue you then?"

He reached out to stroke her cheek, and she held herself still at his touch. "You are, so it doesn't matter."

"That's part of the magic isn't it?" she guessed, pressing the point. "You can only be freed by someone carrying your child because that connection means you can't actually hurt the person when you're a wolf or flame or whatever. Otherwise, you'd kill them."

"A blood tie is needed, yes," he said, sighing as if she were an obstinate child. "It will protect you and I promise I will not cause you any harm."

She was quick to note that he promised he wouldn't hurt her but said nothing of the other elves or Fairy Queen who would probably be furious at having her knight stolen away. And he'd said that they could wed but he'd never promised her that he would. She understood that he'd been manipulating her from the very beginning, trying to maneuver her to serve his own end goal. Any small doubt she had that he wasn't just using her for his own ends evaporated with this realization and that press of desire faded as well, his magic fracturing as she grasped the truth. The strength of his illusions lay in keeping her mind clouded, but now that she was clear-headed she saw through them. His beauty seemed as cold as marble and his eyes cunning and cruel. As if she were seeing him for the first time, she realized that his pallor was corpse-like and his skin cold.

She felt her stomach turning, but she dared not slip up and show her full hand now. She suspected if he realized his enchantment was broken that she'd never leave the Wood alive. She carefully slid the herbs into the pouch at her waist, talking to distract him. "Alright. So you need me to come at midnight and make a holy water circle and pull you from your horse. I don't know when I'd be able to slip away at night, but I could probably come up with a plan in time—"

"No!" he cut in, his handsome face showing just the slightest panic. "No, my pretty Elayne, it's important that you rescue me tonight when the

Court rides. You see it can only be done at the hinges of the year and tonight is Halloween. And it can only be done when the Court rides, which it does tonight. And if you don't, well I'm afraid that next May, when the year turns again, will be too late."

"Too late?" she said, careful to keep her words slow as if she were still confused by his presence. "Why? I'd still have this blood tie to you then."

"You see the Court pays a tithe every year to another Power and it pays with the best of us all," he explained, wincing slightly. "Which is obviously me. So if you do not rescue me tonight then I may be taken...far away. And then what will you do my lovely mortal? With no one to take care of you and no worthy husband?"

He smiled in a way that she was certain was meant to be persuasive, although it seemed empty to her as if he were mimicking what he thought a reassuring smile would look like without being capable of feeling it. She quickly nodded. "Of course. I can see why it must be tonight. That does sound...dire. So I'll go now then. To, ah, prepare myself. For tonight."

He smiled that dazzling smile, his eyes glittering and his face smug. He thought he'd won. "Of course my darling. Don't be afraid. I have complete confidence that you can do this."

"So do I," she agreed, although she was talking about something very different.

With that she slipped free of him and moved back to her horse, trying not to run and give herself away. She mounted and turned, waving slightly at him in farewell. He stood and watched her go, his eyes hooded, his face still smug and triumphant. She knew at some point he'd realize she'd taken the herbs with her and she could only pray she'd be out of the Wood and out of his reach first.

With that thought stuck in her mind, she rode without looking back, her shoulders tight, waiting for him to appear again or try to stop her as she retraced her route out of the woods. She didn't dare urge her horse to run, knowing that would give her away. She didn't relax until she and her sturdy little horse were back on open ground and a mile away from the Wood

When she reached the slight rise—barely a hill—from which she could see the Wood to the north and her father's keep to the south. She stopped her horse for a moment, turning back. As long as she lived, she'd never set foot in it again nor would she mock the stories about its dangers. Reaching down she put her hand on the slight bulge of plants in her pouch, confident that she could prepare them the way that Katherine had advised and that soon she'd be in control of her own destiny again.

He thought he'd won, but he was wrong. She was the one who ruled her own body, not him, and she was the one in control of this situation.

She had no intention of that changing.

A LOVE LIKE CELLOPHANE

EZRA ARNDT

"You don't have to lie."

Don't I?
Are you saying that you won't cut out my tongue if
I don't play your game?
Will I make it through the night if I talk back?

Will you choke me with your love, my lips turning
blue?

Imagine us, my arm linked with yours.
Look at you, all slick and handsome,
your crown of privilege atop your golden curls.
A crown you did nothing to earn.

You broke in, armed with that cocky smile tugging
on your wide mouth.
You pinned me to our bed with a knife to my throat.
You whispered sweet nothings until I gave you
what you wanted so I would keep breathing.

"It wasn't like that."

Wasn't it?
Are you implying that I'm the one who lies to the
authorities' faces?
Would it make a difference if I hadn't said anything
at all?
Would you be forgiving and not be generous with
your violent affection?

Imagine us, your hand tightly encircling mine.
Look at you, tall and strong,
your protective warmth encircling us.
A warmth—my warmth—that you steal from me
every night.

You throw away the covers, lust and rage
intermingling in your once soft eyes.
You leave me exposed to the elements, to the dark
dancing with your shadow.
You told me you wouldn't have to hurt me so much
if I hadn't spoken up.

"I'm not the bad guy."

Aren't you?
Are you claiming that you've never hurt me in any
and every way you could?
Will you let me go peacefully if I decide that I've
had enough?
Will you be a friendly face if our paths ever cross
again?

Imagine us, my body heavy with your children.
Look at you, proud and beaming,
your only trusted possession—a weapon—ready
to defend your family.

A weapon used to hurt me when I speak of my
dreams of being not "woman."
You force a band around my ring finger, promising
me that things will be better this way.
You hold me until my skin bruises and I stay the
same person you loved into submission.
You're a monster, and you expect *me* to carry *your*
babies?

"You can't leave me."

Can't I?
Can I scream in your face and name you the demon
you are without fearing your touch?
Would I be *allowed* to bloom into the person I thirst
to be under your weighty gaze?
Would you support me as I journeyed away from
the predetermined role for me as your wife?

Imagine me, waiting in a sterile room.
Look at me, sobbing and standing straighter than
I'll ever be,
my body purging your uncleanliness.

Uncleanliness that I'll spend the rest of my life
scrubbing away.
I will take nothing with me, naked and afraid for a
future I finally have.
I will not come back even if I turn around as I slip
into the night.
I'll be free from you as soon as the pain in my womb
stops.

BUMPER CROP

SARAH GRACE TUTTLE

When the whisper came, it came from a pumpkin. She had been expecting the whisper, mind you. She just hadn't thought that the spirits would choose a pumpkin as their speakerphone.

"Come out to your garden at midnight," the whisper said. It repeated three times, as if to make sure she got the message. It made the insides of her ears itch.

Her mother, grandmother, and great-grandmother had all heard the whisper—for all she knew, all her mothers had heard it. They told her it would happen. That their family had dealings with spirits. They never quite looked her in the eye when they talked about it.

At midnight, she went outside. The flickering porch lamp startled the shadows of leaves. She walked to the center of the yard and waited. And the choice was offered. And she was grateful.

When she told them what she had done, her mother wailed. What about grandchildren? Her grandmother hung her head. But the spirits had been planning to exact their payment from someone eventually. Why not her? "The difference between me and you," she told them, "is that I don't want to pass debt down the line."

Sometimes, she wondered if the spirits had known that it wouldn't be a sacrifice for her. Sometimes, she wondered what her life would be like if she had chosen differently. Mostly, she enjoyed being able to love without fear.

After that, she always kept a pumpkin on her kitchen table. She liked them. They made her feel free.

Meanwhile, in another garden...

The day she found out she was pregnant, the pumpkin sprouted. She tended it carefully, bending on her knees in the heat and rain to keep it free of weeds and pests—singing to it just as much as she sang to her belly. Sometimes more, if she was honest.

As the vine spread out, she took time every morning to count the leaves on each tendril. She tickled them.

"You touch that vine more than you touch me," her wife grumped.

On nights when pregnancy made her too hot to sleep, she snuck out into the garden and told the pumpkin bedtime stories.

The plant bore just one fruit, and it began to swell. She pet its fuzzy stem, and cradled its body against her own.

Her wife convinced the doctor to come observe her. He shrugged. "Pregnancy brain is strange," he said, watching her feed the ground mashed carrots. "I wouldn't worry."

In her third trimester, she kept a cot in the garden. She would lie there with one hand on the pumpkin's ripening flesh and feel its heartbeat.

When her water broke, the pumpkin split open. There was her child—covered in orange goo, with perfect fingers and toes. Her wife insisted they go to the hospital.

The doctor said she should have come in before she delivered the baby, but both she and the child were fine.

Later, she and her wife sat on the sofa and discussed their future. They both agreed—they needed a much larger garden. More pumpkins.

Meanwhile, in another garden...

The pumpkin appeared in front of her azaleas just before sunset. As she watched, the pumpkin grew and grew, and from its side came a light... and then there was a door, and she stepped through.

They showed her the seeds they could plant for her, and she held each in her hands. Some were too hot, or too cold, or spiky, or sticky... but eventually she found one that was warm, and glimmered, and was both heavy and soft—like a cozy blanket, curled up in the cup of her palm.

"This one," she said.

They touched it to her solar plexus, and she felt the energy vine through her body— shaping it to the future she'd chosen. For a moment, she glowed. And then she was in the garden. And the pumpkin was just a pumpkin.

At first, the changes were subtle. She wore her favorite color of eyeshadow a bit more. Lingered a little longer near flowering trees. Sat on the patio and read a good book when the party got too loud.

Her friends said she seemed off, but she felt as though she were finally stabilizing. Like her roots were sinking into the earth, and she could stretch and sway in the breeze and never fall.

Her mother had notions—marriage and grandchildren and a mother-in-law-apartment added onto a house in the suburbs. Her mother insisted on a blind date with a friend's son. So, she went. She went, and the instant his hand lingered on her hip, she left.

When she told her mother no more dates, a flower unfurled in her chest.

Her home was perfect for one human and heavy tables of plants. She stretched out in the sun, and her breath felt deep and refreshing—like she was so full of life she could breathe out oxygen.

Like she could be content forever.

SPITE OR: MORE HUMAN IN THE GRAVE

ALICE SCOTT

At the age of thirteen, Stanislav Devorak had already encountered death twice and somehow come out the other side.

The first occurred even before he had a name. Some decidedly unforeseen complication in his birth nearly snatched the fifth child of the prestigious Devorak family without giving him a real chance to *live.* It would be many years before his parents would tell him how they'd chosen his name that day. Born and nearly died on a bleak January day, one where the clouds threatened to split apart and loose a blizzard while his parents spent several harrowing hours hoping, wondering, waiting. Doctors both mortal and mage did everything they could, and apparently then they knew if he was meant to die that day, they at least wanted a name to bury him under.

Stanislav, after some absolute battle axe of a great-grandfather he'd never have the chance to meet, in hopes that some ancestral resilience would carry him through.

By some combination of medical science, healings magics, and perhaps the spirit of a dead ancestor, the child managed to survive.

His second near-death was in many ways less dramatic, and at thirteen years old, this time young Stanislav was old enough to understand it.

The rug in the hall sliding out from under his feet and the staircase rushing up to meet him; his head smacking on the wooden edge of the stair, vision white, nausea roiling; a sickening crack-crack-crack *that could've been his head? His leg? His right leg hurt so much, he was certain if he could see he'd find the bone jutting out as he bounced down the stairs like a stone skipped*

*over water; there was blood in his hair, running down
his face, when he finally stopped falling he would've
thought himself dead were it not for his sister screaming
Stas, oh god, Stas; it took far too long to remember that
was his name, the one only his family used for him.*

*He always was a sickly, brittle-boned child, born
under midwinter clouds with one foot in the grave,
something he'd never quite shaken since that day. His
parents would see him lying in a broken heap at the
bottom of the grand staircase and have to wonder once
more if their youngest wasn't meant for this world.*

Doctors and magicians be damned, this time
he could attribute his near-miraculous survival to
spite.

Spite, because the Devorak name held certain
connotations of dignity, influence, and wealth,
of brilliant scholars, gifted magicians, the
embodiment of *power* going back generations. Yet
his only claim to the family name was as *the one
who'd twice beaten death*. Spite, because now he
understood how he scared them, his family, as he
epitomized the great Devorak clan's fallibilities;
they were only as strong as their weakest member,
their poor youngest son who by all accounts
shouldn't have lived to see the spring. Spite,
because when he lay at the bottom of the stairs
more bloody, broken mess than boy, he knew he'd
only ever be the family martyr if he died there:
a memory toted out for sympathy or leverage, a
means to an end, never remembered beyond his
frailty.

And as gloomy weather washed his bedroom in shadow, he let spite rouse him from his bed.

"Hey, hey, off your feet now," Tatiana murmured. His sister rushed to his bedside the way someone would towards a small bird about to fall from its nest too soon. She was seventeen, and despite the years between then, the only one of his plethora of siblings Stas dared consider himself *close* with. Certainly the only one he'd trust with today's request. "You only *just* got the stitches out of your head and probably have some sort of post-concussion—"

"Yes, I'm well aware, which is why I need someone to walk me over to the library wing. 'Someone' in this case being you." His expression could almost be described as perturbed and didn't belong on such a young face.

"You know you're not supposed to be out of bed. You could fall again, your knee—"

"That's why I'm asking you to keep me upright."

"Upright? When you can barely walk as-is?"

He wouldn't give her the satisfaction of seeing him wobble like a baby fawn, and that's why he stayed perched on the edge of his bed. "I have a cane." He gestured to where it leaned against the nightstand.

"That's for helping you walk the *short* distance to the bathroom—" She gestured across the expanse of his room. "—not to go traipsing halfway across the house."

"Exactly, I wouldn't make it over to the library by myself. Hence asking you to keep me upright."

"Why do you..." She huffed, blowing her dark hair away from her face. "You're my baby brother and you still look like you're on death's door. If you get hurt again, I...I can't watch you fight for your life a third time."

"You were four the first time and not there to witness it, I'm sure."

"But how do you think I like *that* being my earliest memory, Stas?" Tatiana asked. "One minute I was hoping maybe this time I'd get a sister and the next...I don't remember when Niko was born, did you know that? I was too young then, and it's been so overshadowed by the fact that we almost lost you before I ever got to meet you. So I'm going to worry, does that make sense? Please say it makes sense."

Stas hated how she begged him to understand, how they both knew what he considered sensical was often an enigma to everyone else. He wouldn't meet Tatiana's gaze, focusing instead on the brace on his battered leg: sleek lines of metal and leather, annoyingly stylized lest a *Devorak* of all people be mistaken for a Dickensian urchin, and stamped with an overabundance of sigils meant to help him walk, keep him healing, ease the pain of his ruined bones.

After the fall, his eldest brothers hadn't even bothered to check if he'd actually fallen asleep before having their hushed conversations in the hall outside his room. Apparently, his knee had shattered so severely that neither magic nor the metal pins holding him together now could fix him entirely; he'd always have something of a limp, an ache on days like this where the pressure in the air changed, a knee that wouldn't straighten out like it should. One whispered that now Stas would have even more trouble keeping up with the rest of the family, the other agreed it was foolish for him to ever try to begin with.

They didn't entirely mean his gait.

Spite.

"It makes sense," he murmured. "But I feel like I'm waiting for death to try a third time, with a family that thinks I'm too frail to exist. I'm not asking for some wild adventure; I just need a literal shoulder to lean on while we walk to the library. I'm bored, Tati, and nobody seems to get that: how I don't want to sit in bed with nothing to do but watch the snow come down and wait to die. Nobody else gets *me*, they didn't before the fall, and they don't now."

Was it underhanded? Perhaps. Tatiana had always nurtured a hole in her heart in the shape of him, and Stas had realized that when he was old enough to understand just how touch and go it had been almost thirteen years ago exactly. He could press and she would fold, especially if he added that nickname only he used for her.

"Get your cane." Tatiana sighed. "On the condition that if you start having concussion side effects, you tell me immediately and stop reading."

"Fine," he said, intending for less immediacy than she would surely like.

"*And* when I tell you it's time to stop and come back for your medicine, you won't fight me?"

Hmm.

"*Stas*," she prompted at his hesitation.

"Okay."

He picked up his cane from its spot against the nightstand as Tatiana offered her elbow like the hero of a period piece.

Their pace pained him, more so than just his injury. The family home—the *estate*, rather, no fool would call this place something as quaint as a home—often felt less like a place for a family to grow and more like a menagerie for five children poised to inherit the world: a massive, extravagant cage. Stas hated lingering anywhere outside his room, out where the family opulence was on full display. How his eldest brothers, proper adults with college degrees and the potential for freedom, could stand to come back here at the end of each day when a whole world waited for them, he would never understand.

Perhaps the estate was simply more inviting when you weren't the family revenant. Ironic how he, the one most desperate to leave, was the one whose body saw fit to clip his wings before he ever had a chance.

That very reason had prompted this trip to the library. He hadn't *technically* lied; he didn't have any interest in sitting in bed, waiting for something else to go wrong, though it wasn't the entire reason.

The Devorak family library was the culmination of generations worth of knowledge on the arcane, the scientific, and every conceivable overlap. His best chance at finding anything helpful would be there, and Tatiana was too good for him to drag her into his rabbit hole of research. The look on her face with every wince he bit back told him everything he needed to know about the words she swallowed. If he gave any indication of faltering, she would surely stop, haul him into her arms if need be and carry him back to his room. Hell, she'd probably offer to bring books back and read them aloud to him to keep from straining his already injured brain. She didn't need to know what it was he sought in that vast array of tomes, telling her without something to show for it would only cause more concern. He'd happily let her think his intentions lay solely with staving off bedridden boredom, killing time.

At least for now, all he had was time.

They spent that afternoon in relative silence, the only sound the crackling of the grand fireplace in an attempt to stave off the chill. Stas sat on the floor, a hoard of old books encircling him and his injured leg propped up on a cushion. He scribbled madly in the notebooks spread across the floor, a pen in each hand. All the while, Tatiana perched on a chaise and measured the hours in the snow piling on the windowsill, pretending to study the antiques on the shelves or family portraits on the walls whenever Stas caught her watching him with abject concern. Occasionally he'd point out books too high on the shelf for him to reach, asking her to retrieve them and knowing each time she'd ask if he was *sure* he wouldn't prefer to sit somewhere more comfortable than the floor. His answer never changed.

"All right, you've been staring at those books so long it's making *my* head hurt, and I think it's almost time for your pills, up you go," Tatiana said finally. Stas remained on the floor until she handed him his cane, gathering his spread of notebooks and tucking them under one arm. "I'll put the books back once I get you settled, but you did promise you wouldn't fight me on this."

"I suppose I did," Stas muttered, allowing his sister to ease him to his feet. "You're correct."

"And *you* are the most formal thirteen-year-old I've ever met," Tatiana said. "You're so proper, like a little librarian."

"I'm *direct*."

"Which is a way of saying you're an old man in the body of a teenage boy."

"Vlad and Andrey would likely say you're correct, I do have the brittle bones of a geriatric."

"You aren't helping your case when you use words like *geriatric*, but yes, the twins can be…unintentionally cruel." Tatiana shrugged. "They love you, though, they all do. They're just…scared."

"If you look at me funny, I get a nosebleed for a distressingly long amount of time and the twins are adult men. Vlad is getting a master's degree. I don't see how they could be scared of me."

"Not *of* you, Stas, for you. Look around, look at all our family has; all this money and power and we've still almost lost you twice. This is going to sound terrible, don't hold it against me, but things like that aren't supposed to happen to people like us. I know, *I know*, but allegedly we're wealthy enough to throw a ridiculous amount of money at any problems that arise. That kind of influence gives us a leg up—" Her whole body cringed. "—Sorry, poor choice of words."

"Because of my leg? I wasn't offended," Stas said. "But what I'm hearing is: the world is at our family's fingertips and they still can't find a way to fix me. They don't understand me."

Spite.

"I promise, that's not what I meant."

"I'd like to change the subject now," said Stas, his head throbbed and the last thing he wanted was for her to realize that.

"Okay, new subject. What are all these notes for?" Tatiana asked. "Are you looking for something specific?"

"Not particularly," he lied. "Just what's interesting, so I have something to look over when everyone else forces me to stay in bed. It's better than sitting around dying of boredom."

"Poor choice of words, Stas."

"I'm the one who nearly died, I think I'm allowed to say it."

Days crept by much like this. Tatiana returned each day, probably with the knowledge that if she didn't come back and offer to walk him to the library, he was stubborn enough to shuffle down there on his own and risk further injury. Stas appreciated her presence, mainly because she could navigate the rolling ladder to the higher shelves, something he and his awkward leg still wouldn't risk. He learned not to argue when she told him to drink water or insisted he wrap up for the day and take his medication, and she learned not to further inquire about the contents of his frenzied notes. The singular time she'd asked, he'd stammered a repetitive non-answer.

Time passed and winter kept its gray hold on the estate; each day in the library was spent huddled around the fireplace in a way that could almost be described as cozy, were it not for the older, more precarious tomes Stas had begun to request from darker corners of shelves. Tatiana didn't question it, presumably, she was just delighted to see him enthusiastic about something. She didn't see the desperation in the frantic scribble of his notes, or perhaps she just didn't want to see it, but it kept her from asking what it was he searched for in this absolute well of knowledge.

Even if it left her unprepared when he actually found it.

"Tatiana! Tati, I—" Stas' excitement broke off into a horrible fit of coughing that sent Tatiana shooting to her feet. "I'm fine, I'm fine—" *Cough* "—I just got too excited—" *Cough* "—Really, I'm okay." The dry rasp echoing from his throat painfully contradicted his words.

"You don't sound fine."

"You don't need to worry about my cough," Stas said, bulldozing right past her attempts to correct him. "You won't need to worry about *me*. I found it!"

"Found...what?"

"Exactly what I was hoping for!" Stas beamed. He hefted an old, leather-bound book up like a prize-winning chicken, the print on the page so small and cramped with handwritten notes in the margins that Tatiana couldn't make out its contents. "You said it yourself, our family has all this wealth and power and still I've almost died twice, so it stands to reason there's something we're not seeing, yes? That's what I thought anyway, and it turns out I was right."

"Stas, I adore you, I love how excited you get even when I'm worried you're going to give yourself an asthma attack, but I need you to take a moment. I don't live inside your head; I'm missing some key info here."

"Magic as we use it—the broad we, not our family specifically—is something like a candle.

You light it when you need it and snuff it out
when you're done, dormant and cold when not in
use. It's why the family doctors could use magic
to fit the puzzle pieces of my knee back together,
but that doesn't fix the underlying brittle bones,
those are continual, chronic. But this?" He hiked
up his pant leg, gesturing to the sigils stamped
into his brace. "Is also continual, charmed to
keep the pain manageable and let me walk on it,
because whatever exorbitantly expensive crafter
our parents paid for it managed to imbue the brace
itself with magic. It's so simple, I'm ashamed I
didn't realize this was an option sooner."

"What option?" He bristled at the edge in
Tatiana's voice, the skepticism. The barest hint of
fear.

Spite.

"We've established that highly skilled magical
craftsmen can imbue an inanimate object with
a small fraction of their own power, be it some
sort of charm, or ward, or...or my leg brace for
example!" Even he could tell how positively manic
he sounded, giddy in a way so antithetical to
his usual emotional restraint. Confusion played
across Tatiana's face and he didn't care; she could
be confused now, but she'd be grateful later.
"Wouldn't it make sense if there was a way to...cut
out the middleman, the charm or the sigil, and
make the person themselves the conduit for their
own continual magic? Pop the seal on that power
capability, never snuff the candle out, constantly

let it burn low! Obviously, the power output wouldn't be enough to fix *all* my chronic health problems and assorted comorbidities, certainly my knee is going to be fucked for the rest of my life—"

"I feel like I should tell you not to use that kind of language—"

"—But it would keep everything *manageable!* Especially in combination with the medication! If I can figure out how to do this, tap into my magic, and keep it constantly within reach, I could...I could exist! I wouldn't have to sit in bed all day lest a strong wind breaks my bones, or take pills in the double digits every day; I believe this could certainly clear up the concussion, because who better to go magically rooting around in my brain than *me!* You and everyone else wouldn't have to worry about me so much!"

"Stas—"

If he heard her, he didn't acknowledge it. "Despite being the family pariah, I *am* still a Devorak, and the amount of raw power this family holds is astounding. I can only imagine how much stronger I would be if I did this. It mentions—vaguely, I needed to extrapolate, simple enough—that keeping one's magic constant, not having to call it up from dormancy every time, exponentially increases the raw power. See?" Stas jammed the book into her hands and pointed to one such handwritten note scribbled amongst the printed text.

Magic, above all things, is not an animal; jam it in a cage and it will atrophy, give it freedom to roam and it will come alive.

"There's a number of notes like that, suggesting some sort of, hm, process whoever had this book before we used it, but it seems to have worked for others! I could be powerful, a—"

"A loaded weapon with the safety turned off?" Tatiana interrupted.

"I was going to say a proper person, there's definitely a more apt metaphor than yours," Stas said.

"No, I—you've just told me you want our family to sit back and risk letting you blow your brains out trying to turn your magic into a loaded gun because you *think* it's worked before? Stas, I'm sorry, but no. Let's get you back to bed."

He hadn't expected her to balk like this, to look well and truly afraid.

It always came back to fear, didn't it?

"Where is this coming from?" Stas asked. He needed to know she was the one he couldn't scare.

"I know you have trouble with tone sometimes, but you can't honestly be surprised I'm not keen on this," Tatiana said. "If this worked for whoever made those notes, why is their book in *our* family library? Why haven't we heard about this sort of thing? I feel if this were a Legitimate Option—" Stas could practically hear the arbitrary capitalization, "then it would've been brought up by, say, one of our family's magically inclined doctors, not noted in some unfamiliar grimoire in a dusty corner of the library? Would you say that's a logical leap to make?"

"It's not a *grimoire*, it has *typeface*," Stas insisted.

"You're being too literal again."

"Then help me understand!" Stas begged. "You said it yourself, you're worried about me, the whole family is worried about me, and I'm trying to help! I'm trying to do something so you don't have to be so scared!"

"Do...do you really think we *shouldn't* be scared? You're barely a teenager, and you want us to let you try some sort of back-alley self-surgery for power?"

"I'm not after *power*, and it wouldn't be back-alley surgery. Maybe it would be if I let one of our brothers go rifling through my magic, but I trust myself!"

"That aside, what does your book say to do? Is there a specific recipe for unlocking magic? Any of those handwritten notes explicitly mention a successful outcome? Tell me your plan."

"Like I said, it's a lot of...extrapolation..." Stas started, sounding as frail and small as they all thought him to be. He couldn't let them be right. *Spite.* "But there are mentions of 'putting oneself into a temporary state in which the magic automatically takes over, the way one blinks and breathes without having to make note of it,' so I would assume it would take some sort of lucid dreaming—"

"Mentions, assuming, some sort, I'm hearing a lot of hedging. I don't want to be responsible for, at best, you giving yourself magical sleep paralysis."

"Didn't *you* tell me our family is exceedingly powerful? With all the reading I've been doing, cross-referenced across multiple accounts, I have ideas! I have notes, see!" He gestured to the notebooks on the floor.

"You said those weren't anything in particular, just for bedtime reading."

"Well of course I'm going to go over my ideas later, looking at it with a clear perspective is what let me have a breakthrough—"

"Give me the book, Stas."

"...What?" Stas said. "I mean, I have my notes, but—"

"*Please*, give me the book. I don't know if our mother and father even know it's in here, and at the very least I don't think they'd want you finding it no matter what if this is what you're planning."

"But imagine how thrilled they'd be if I managed to achieve something for myself! I could...contribute something to this family, beyond just being a source of worry! It makes sense! They wouldn't have to be scared!"

"You're scaring me *now*, Stanislav!" Tatiana snapped, his full first name echoing off the high shelves of the room. "You're thirteen and you've got this Dr. Frankenstein giddiness at the prospect of doing something vague and risky and—you could get yourself killed and you only think it sounds like a good idea because you are *thirteen!* You aren't a professional, you aren't a prodigy, you're an understandably scared, frail kid forcing me to be the bad guy because I'm telling you not to risk your life on an *extrapolation!*"

Frail. It always came back to frail.

Spite.

"I don't want to die, Tatiana! I've never wanted to die!" he shouted back. He meant it to sound declarative and he hated the way his voice broke, and the words came out scared. If she thought he was scared, she had no reason not to be. "But that's all everyone sees when they look at me, the boy waiting for an early death that feels inevitable to all of them except for me! I know they must think I'm a burden because I'm–I'm a mess, a disappointment, nothing worth bragging about!" It came out as almost a hiccup and he told himself then, he would *not* cry. "Did you know Mom once told me I scare her because she doesn't think I'm cut out for the world? That she thought that was a perfectly fine thing to tell a child to their face? I scare them, I scare you, and don't clarify *of* me, *for* me, it doesn't matter!"

"I..." A look of icy realization crossed Tatiana's face. "I'm not scared of you, Stas—"

"You just said I'm scaring you," Stas pointed out. "I scare Mom because she's failed as a parent if I can't 'handle the real world,' whatever that means. They talk about 'if there's something wrong, Stas, we'll find a way to fix it,' or something like that."

Tatiana opened her mouth to argue as soon as he said *fix*, but he didn't give her the chance. "But half the time I don't know if they mean my health or the way my mind works, because I know I'm not perfect and glowing like the rest of this family. I turned out *wrong*, with the way I talk and overthink but don't understand everyone else; my mind is working overtime to compensate for the fact that this body that's apparently mine barely works at all, I'm *wrong* and I've known this my whole life! So *please* try to understand *me* when I say that if I have the choice between doing something for myself—something that could make me happier, make my life a little easier, something that would let me live *at all*—and keeping our family from being afraid, I'm going to choose myself! They're already scared, and just maybe I'll be a bit less of a burden if I'm at least a little better off."

Tatiana looked at him like he'd slapped her with the word burden, and belatedly he wondered if he'd crossed a line. He practically panted now, out of breath from the screaming match they'd just finished. "Please, Tati, let me tr—"

The sentence died when he doubled over coughing again, a ragged sound that shook his whole skinny frame. Of course. Of course, he couldn't stand up for himself for one pathetic moment without being undermined by the frailty they all saw when they looked at him.

"Stas?" Tatiana whimpered, kneeling beside him. "Stas, say something."

But he didn't, no matter how badly he wanted to. He just kept coughing.

"Stanislav!" He weakly held up a hand, their universal if rarely believed gesture for *it'll pass.* "Fuck I'm…" She didn't say anything else, just grabbed the book he'd been holding and ran from the library, in search of their parents or the twins, someone with a modicum of authority who could manage a crisis.

Fine, he could work without the book; it wasn't ideal, but he had notes. Swallowing back the coughing fit, forcing it to subside by will alone, he hobbled to the library door and locked it. That would keep Tatiana and the cavalry out at least a little bit longer.

What had the book said? *A state in which the magic automatically takes over, the way one blinks and breathes without having to make note of it?* The way the body remembered its need for air when one passed out from holding their breath? Stas didn't have time for anything close to lucid dreaming, but he could expedite the timeline of passing out if needed.

One thing he was keenly aware of since his head had split open on the stairs and it had poured down his face, was that he had quite a lot of blood to lose.

He sat back down beside the fireplace, the midwinter wind howling outside like an omen, and rolled up his pant leg again.

This leg was fucked no matter what, right?

Spite.

Reality moved at triple speed as Stas pitched
forward with a shuddering gasp, looking very much
like someone awakened from the dead to the
assembled crowd. His parents, his sister, they'd
all gathered like a funeral procession. His mouth
tasted like pennies; somewhere between that first
cut and passing out, his nose had begun to bleed
as well, spattering on his notes. As long as they
were still readable, he didn't care. He didn't bother
lingering on his family members to gauge their
reactions, their *fear*. He stared instead at the bloody
piece of metal gripped in his hand, one of the
admittedly more decorative pieces of his leg brace
he'd managed to snap off. He glanced between it
and the damage done to his leg. The damage *he* had
done.

Truthfully, he'd barely registered that his family
was there at all until he heard them gasp.

"Stas, what did you do?"

Tatiana spoke with a whispered mixture of
horror and reverence, like she'd thought the third
time was the charm and this had finally killed
him. Her reaction didn't particularly surprise him;

he hadn't known what shape this upheaval would take. The texts were vague on the after. He held out his hand, watching his veins glow purple like an aurora beneath his skin. Violet light skittered across the wound on his leg, beginning to stitch it closed. Obvious power thrummed in his new, if admittedly feeble magic; this would definitely leave another scar. He'd have to make note of these particular aftereffects if he could find an unbloodied page in his journals.

"I told you," Stas said, looking up at his sister with a perfectly calm expression. Not until much later would he find out their looks of terror were because his eyes also glowed, the normally brown irises ringed in purple light, eyes like a predator in the dark. Without the crackle of the fire, the library was as quiet as the grave.

"I chose myself this time."

Devorak family holidays were embodiments of the excess the family had become known for, breeding grounds for painful small talk, and in his twenty-five years, Stanislav Devorak had never gotten particularly good at navigating them. The

New Year's Eve party that swept through the halls would've been a joyous occasion if Stas hadn't known better: his family could dress the new year up in lights and music and drink, but it was always the frostbitten herald that his birthday was only weeks away.

And with his birthday came the bitter chill of the anniversary of his accident, when his head had split, his knee had shattered, and he'd gotten the terrible idea to finally choose his own quality of life. Stas saw through the party for what it was: a distraction as so many were, and any event that summoned him back to his family estate usually resulted in hiding in the library.

"Avoiding our family?" Tatiana's voice pulled him from his thoughts.

"Not necessarily," he lied.

Looking at her, he almost laughed at their unintentionally coordinated clothes: both of them dressed in button-ups and fitted vests, all in shades of black and purple. An unintentional uniform for the Devorak family's two token queers. Tatiana, though, looked like some sort of corvid queen with a skirt that kissed her ankles and her shiny black hair fanning out behind her.

Stas, with his faded scars and dark circles under his eyes, wished, not for the first time and not for the last, that he'd grown up as beautiful as his sister.

He'd perched himself on the benchlike brick edge of the library's fireplace, several rooms away from the party. The fire crackled at his back as he absently rubbed his knee, his injured leg thrown over the other.

"Can I join you at the very least?" Tatiana asked.

Wordlessly, Stas moved his cane away from the spot beside him on the fireplace. "How did you know where to find me?"

"You've got a flair for both the dramatic and the ironic; no matter how many years it's been since you moved out, I know to check here first." She glanced down. The carpet was red to begin with, and after over a decade of cleanings, any phantom stains of Stas' blood from that day probably only existed in their heads. There had been so much blood. "Does it still hurt?"

"The knee? Not as much. It aches when the weather is bad, or if I've been on my feet too long, but the brace helps and it's so much better than it would've been, had I not...intervened," Stas mused. "But the scar? Never."

"I shouldn't have run off that day," Tatiana said, nudging the carpet with the toe of her boot.

"So you've said, many times over the years," said Stas. No malice colored his words, just a simple, flat statement of facts. "And I've told you just as many times that I don't hold it against you. If anything, I'm glad you did. It gave me the opportunity."

Tatiana winced. "Can I ask you something, if we're talking about that day?"

"Are we?"

"Why did you do it?"

Spite.

Stas looked at her now, the concern as plain on her face as it had been that day. He could still remember her pained expression even now.

He supposed tonight *would* be a night to keep rehashing old conversations.

"I feel as though I've answered that countless times to one sibling or another," he said.

"Still talking like an old man, huh?" Tatiana laughed.

"I am old now. It's fitting."

"You're twenty-five."

"And I have lived lifetimes in those two and a half decades, Tati." He sighed. "If you want to know why I'm hiding out here, it's the same reason it always is: I'm a jaded bastard who doesn't socialize well, I can feel everyone's relief when I leave the room, they can speak more freely even as they look down on me for being antisocial. I scare them, I always have, the only difference now is they're justified. I did, what did you call it? Back-alley surgery on my own magic? And to them, any type of power that takes that to unlock *must* be inherently dangerous, evil, consuming."

He held out his hand, watching his veins pulse and glow violet for a moment before the magic—that raw, unrestrained thing always waiting just below the surface—settled back down beneath his skin.

"Was it worth it?" Tatiana asked.

"Absolutely," Stas said, without hesitation. "You ask me why when I told you why the day it happened: I wasn't risking death again, so I chose myself. I wanted to be stronger, I wanted to *live*. It was a gamble, but they'd be scared of me anyway, I'd rather give them a reason and live as I please, and oh, I've *lived*. Look at me now, look at what constant low-level healing magic can do." He gestured to himself, willing her to look past the perpetual dark circles from late nights and the hollow of his cheekbones, to see instead the light in his eyes, the genuine smile on his face.

"I don't bleed for so long, it doesn't feel like my bones will break if I look at them funny, it fixed the post-concussion syndrome right away. I'm not perfect but I'm better, so much better than that boy who could never quite get out from under the shadow of dying the day I was born, forever haunted, forever sick. I took matters into my own hands to protect myself and...I think our family vilifies me for it. I hold immense power, but I've only ever used it in combination with my medication to mitigate the rotten hand I was dealt with my health. I don't think this makes me the villain here, wanting to live, but..." He shook his head. "I've made peace with our brothers, our parents, and now we can all be civil and kind to one another, but they'll only ever see me as a firearm in a child's hands."

"I shouldn't have called you a loaded gun that day," Tatiana said, putting her hand on Stas' knee.

"I know I've apologized for leaving and for yelling so many times since then, but I don't think I've ever apologized for that."

"You haven't," Stas said, another simple statement of fact. "But they would've thought of me that way even if you hadn't put it into those words. They think of this magic as some kind of terrible thing, something inhuman, and I've paid its tithe in blood. They're certain I can't control the newfound magnitude of my magic, or that perhaps it's sentient and is just biding its time until it can possess me or what have you. It *isn't* sentient, my mind is no different with it than I was before, but they can blame their changeling fantasy on it because it's easier to say I played with magic too strong for me than for them to admit I'm autistic." He laughed, so softly it was mostly to himself. "Because when I didn't have to worry about my body as much, I lived long enough to put a word to what's going on with my mind. It's *freeing*.

"And in the years since I've thought about your loaded gun comment, and didn't I say then that there's probably a more apt metaphor?"

"Did you come up with something?"

Stas nodded. "I think so. Most magicians use their magic like a candle, light it when you need it, enjoy the light and warmth, let it sit cold until it's needed again. That day in the library I didn't light a candle, I turned on a whole gas stove. There's potential for so much more fire than what people expect magic to be, so much more power, but it's also about what I do with it: I can warm my hands, cook a meal and provide the sustenance to survive another day, or I can strike a match and let everything explode, burn the whole world down. I just have to understand myself well enough to know when and where to handle the flames."

Tatiana fell silent, and he watched her take this in, taking the opportunity to continue his train of thought. "And I'll tell *you* because I'm fairly certain you're the only one with even a chance of believing me: I have no interest in lighting matches. If this kind of magic exists, why did I find out about it scribbled in a book our parents bought at an estate sale? I want to *study* it, not...abuse it. Everyone who is supposed to love me already fears me enough as it is."

"They *do* love you..."

"I know they do, truly, but I also know that I *do* scare them. They'll throw money at my research and in return, I keep to myself, don't try wielding my magic like a weapon to take over the world, so they don't have to explain the monster their youngest son made of himself." Stas drummed his fingers on his leg, the one that would never be quite right again. "No matter how many times I tell them that it doesn't interest me at all, they'll always see a monster because they can't understand me, why I would do what I did. I'm probably alive today because of that reckless gamble I took as a child, would I be more human in the grave? Less of something to fear had I sat so prettily and waited to die? Made myself the Devorak martyr, accepted that as my fate?"

He turned towards her and let the magic crash over him, reaching it like an outstretched hand. Watching his eyes ring purple surely reminded her of *that* day in awful, vivid detail. "Are you afraid of me, Tati? We've made our peace since then, but you're the only one I'm still unsure about. I won't be offended if you say yes."

This is where she'd admit yes, she'd always been afraid in some shape or form, for him or of him, it didn't matter. At best, she'd tell him to *please stop glowing*, at worst she'd run back to the safety of the party, but at the very least she'd—

—hug him.

Tatiana threw her arms around her brother, pulled him close. Not the pitiful, halfhearted hug of his eldest brothers who thought they'd break him, not the brief one-armed thing of everyone afraid unrestrained magic to be catchable. A real hug.

"No," she mumbled into his hair. "I worry about you but I refuse to be afraid of you. More human in the grave, that's—you'll always be my baby brother, I want you alive, whatever form that may take. As long as I don't have to walk in and find you in a puddle of your own blood again, then I can promise not to fear you. Even if no one else in our family can say the same, I will always love you."

Stas always hated this time of year. He was thin enough to always be cold, and the rapid succession of anniversaries of his birth, his accident, and his ritual, every time he'd fought for his life crammed in the space of one frigid winter were enough to make him write off the whole season. But for the first time in over a decade, the winter would bring something he could hold with fondness. He couldn't tell her that, couldn't risk letting his emotions get the better of him, risk admitting how badly he needed to hear that: the blessing to be, not as the monster who saw no qualms with slicing open his own leg, not as the loaded gun, not as the horror everyone saw because they didn't understand his mind, but as the man who wanted to live.

Monster. Changeling. Inhuman Thing. Whatever villain his family made of him be damned. He knew the truth, knew he'd never felt more alive.

All Stanislav Devorak had ever wanted was to be allowed to live.

IMMUTABLE

MORGAN DAIMLER

My eyes are not your mirror, reflecting
   what you want
   me to become.
   Long before you there were others trying
   to break me,
   to shape me.
   I am a river flowing freely, wearing down
   obstacles,

bursting boundaries.
I am a flame searing to ash my own dross,
bright burning,
relentless.
I am the dark, deep, inescapable night that
cannot be
contained.
If you think of me as a dream, don't mistake me
for the sort
you wish for;
Unless you wish for wilderness and wild things,
the smell of
copper and rain.
Do not think to make me into what you desire.
I am fierce.
I am powerful.
An Otherworldly force moves within me.
I am myself;
immutable.

FIREBIRD

SAM AMENN

Wretched grasping.
They needed a host.
I burned away.
Neither wanted to die.
Neither expected to survive.

It began with a special mission, the kind they used
to get all the time on Earth. Go where you're not

wanted, rescue those who are too terrified to be saved, and try not to die in the process. On Earth, it would have been a team of eight: a driver, two doctors, and the rest mercenaries. This time it would only be Grigori the Slavic Robocop, Ruslan, the doctor who still thought it was possible to be good in this slaughterhouse called existence, and a handful of terrified X'ythalians soldiers. Their scientific counterparts were mysteriously dying on a remote planet and their X'ythalian queen thought maybe the "hoomans" could figure it out.

A *good luck* from Bronislava, their sentient AI housed in their ship and under their skin, as the X'ythalian ship doors closed. The rest of their team of "hoomans" and AI held back, reserved for a mission of greater importance.

They all hated being separated; shot into the dark unknown with only Bronislava to keep them tethered to each other.

But even Bronislava had limits.

Immediately upon arriving on the planet both Ruslan and Grigori agreed: something wasn't right. But that's the way it always is. Investigation, a dark secret uncovered, now what?

Ruslan went to talk to Allah while Grigori hatched a plan with help from Bronislava several parsecs away, her reach weak.

An explosion.

Ringing.
The world turned upside down
Flying.
Crashing.
Agony and the death rattle.
Grigori! Grigori!
Bronislava called in his mind, but her spark grew
ever fainter as if they were being pulled away.
Replaced by something else.
Something desperate and terrified. Something that
clung to him like emerald fire to oil, coating
his insides and outsides, silencing his mind,
consuming him whole until he *was* the emerald
inferno.
Existence was unformed and yet they recognized
each other instantly. Two beings separated by
the entire universe, but maybe the gap could
be crossed. Maybe communication was possible
under the right circumstances.

Grigori brought a mechanical hand to his eyes to
shade them from the fiery red light of the setting
sun flirting through Ruslan's glass doors. The last
rays of light brushing across the marble tile and

white brick walls of his living room in his French townhouse. The garden just a step away. Faint noise from the kitchen and in a second Ruslan would emerge, carrying two wine glasses.

The soft fabric of Ruslan's couch nearly consumed Grigori as he sipped his wine, his heart racing, painfully aware how warm Ruslan's thigh felt pressed against his, a movie droning on in the background. It didn't matter which one. Grigori stole a glance at Ruslan in his ridiculous white suit and his gray, "distinguished" sideburns, gesturing at the screen and sharing a film fact. His brown skin positively glowing when compared to Grigori's pasty white skin.

Grigori looked down and frowned at his own outfit. It was the wrong one.

He wore his black tube top that allowed his mechanical arms to move without snagging on any fabric, his flannel skirt, black tights, and black combat boots at the club, not dinner. He was probably wearing his thick and heavy eyeliner as well. Ruslan claimed that Slavic men pulled off the gothic look best.

Grigori shook his head, his dirty blonde bangs tumbling into his face. No, this wasn't right. None of this was right. Two different moments happening at once.

"Relax. This will only work if you're comfortable."

The thought was in Ruslan's voice, the Uzbek accent warm and familiar, and it pulled Grigori back to this moment, this peace, quiet, and

security. Ruslan asked a question and even though
Grigori didn't understand what it was, his mouth
and tongue moved of their own accord.

Grigori: If there was a time before the war, I don't
remember it. My first memory is of my mother's
red, left sneaker in my hands. What remained
of her lined the smoking crater before me. My
father screaming, tugging on my jacket, until he
fell beside me. The back of his head twisted around
a piece of hot metal. I was thirteen.

*Not Ruslan: I didn't have a "mother" or "father", not
like you. Only a creator and me, their shard. Our captors
created me by forcing my creator to reach an energy
level of a small nuclear bomb and then forced that
energy inward, tearing them in two. They used nullifying
tongs to pull me out of the container while my creator
withered on the bottom of their prison, their particles
coming together to form a tendril that reached out to
me.*

Grigori: I crawled into the crater that was my
mother and wrapped myself around her shoe,
waiting to die. The bombardments lasted all day
and all night, but never found me. Not the delayed
crumble of a building gutted by a rocket. Not the
snap snap snap of cluster bombs dancing across
what remained of the roads. Not the screaming
strikes of the incendiary bombs that rained from
the sky, lighting half-demolished blocks on fire. I

prayed to my parents' ghosts, "Please, just let me die."

> *Not Ruslan: My captors were beings with a fixed physical form, with pinchers for mouths, six eyes, four arms. Their bodies were part grayish flesh, part machines that hummed with a familiar presence. My creator's presence. Shattered to glowing particles, unable to think or react on its own, burning away to almost nothing to keep my captors alive. I tried to reach out to my creator's pieces, but they were too weak to respond. My captors shoved me into a tight prison void of light, sound, and air, the vague cry of my creator cut off as soon as they closed the door. I was completely alone.*

Grigori: The Silver Wolves found me, the drone dogs built by the Americans and sold to the highest bidders before the war. They grabbed me by the ankle and pulled me out of the crater. I lost my mother's shoe as I screamed and clawed at the debris. The moment I latched onto something solid, the wolf broke my ankle clean in two and there was only pain. Three wolves guarded me until the unshaven, unwashed, drunk soldiers found me. Their officer let them use me as needed for a few hours before snapping at them to leave me alone. That I was marked to be sent to Polygon II.

Ruslan was gone and Grigori rose, the living room falling away with each step, revealing nothing but darkness. The eternal night collapsed onto his shoulders as the last wall crumbled away. He screamed as he collapsed to his knees, not because it hurt, but because it *should* have hurt. His mechanical hands were impossibly silent as he pushed against the relentless darkness. A faint echo of a pounding heart and the ticklish memory of sweat down his face as he fought for a life wasn't convinced he still had. Another mechanical cry as he collapsed face down into the darkness.

Dead?

No, rotating until he was right side up, the darkness pinning him in a spot, as if he was in a coffin, his arms futilely pushing against the invisible walls.

Not Ruslan: I wasted so much time throwing myself at the cool, dark walls, spinning around endlessly as if I'd find a new part of my prison, even begging pathetically for my creator or my captors to help me. At my most desperate, I drew myself together, daring to vibrate and burn until nothing remained, but I wasn't strong enough. I only glowed brighter, but never enough to hurt anyone. I vibrated fast enough to produce sparks, but not enough to burn the prison to the ground. I was a coward. Too afraid of dying to generate the strength needed to escape.

He gasped as his hands froze against the lid, his metal fingers sparking with energy as something invisible intertwined with them. From his hands emerged emerald-green particles, expanding until they matched the dimensions of his own form. The cluster of particles swarmed in a circular pattern like plankton. It expanded and contracted at will, flashing with whatever emotion was running through it as it spoke. It was beautiful like a flame is beautiful to a moth.

Grigori: What is this? What are you?

Not Ruslan: Don't stop sharing! The mindspace isn't stable yet.

Grigori: Mindspace?

Not Ruslan: Please! We can only build it together. I don't fully understand, but our memories strengthen it. Tell me what happened in Polygon II.

Grigori: They handed me to the Devil. Captain Anatoli Marinov of the Enhanced Weaponry Division. His own men called him Koschei the Deathless behind his back while his subjects always called him the Bear. He lined thirteen of us up and inspected us personally. When he came to me, I was standing on my broken ankle, my cheek swollen because a soldier punched me for resisting him. His aide told him the story and Marinov smiled, baring his teeth like a wolf about to strike. He patted my bruised cheek and said, "This one."

I was the only child pulled out of line. When he finished his inspection, he placed his large hand on my shoulder and directed me into the complex as his soldiers opened fire on those left behind.

Not Ruslan: Devil. Koschei. So many words for evil. I did not face my devils until long after my birth when my prison moved. I had forgotten it was possible, that there was another world outside my dark cage. That there were other beings besides me. The movement was constant and disorienting and I grew to hate it as much as I hated the stillness. When it stopped, I begged them not to leave me. A hiss answered my cries and one of the walls slid open and I felt a different darkness. One that was warm and still sparked of another being, one like me. I shot forward, not thinking, not caring.
It was a bigger container, clear so I could look upon my clicking, clacking captors bound to the black suits keeping them alive, with their meters and measurements and notes, their silent machines. Silent until the door to my new prison slid closed and then excruciating pain as if my entire body was on fire and pieces of myself flew into their wires and into their machines which churned, creaked, and beeped and parts of myself traveled further than that and I understood. The warm fragments of the other being were all that remained. They had burnt them to the point of extinction. I was their replacement.

Grigori: I'm sorry. I knew as soon as Ruslan and I found you, even before we touched. We wanted to help...

Not Ruslan: Keep sharing. Our bond is almost complete.

Grigori: Bond? What bond?

Not Ruslan: Marinov, Grigori, what did Marinov want with you?

Grigori: It wasn't clear at first. Just a number of tests, training, and examinations. Over and over again. Run, climb, fight, sit still, draw your blood, check your vitals, memorize this, learn that, repeat after me. Don't you know you're being prepared for a greater purpose? And that bastard, Marinov, hiding in the shadows, watching all.

Let me lead minor revolts because he wanted to see how far we would get before his own men could bring us down. The first time we didn't even leave our rooms before they beat us into submission. The second time, we got to the end of the hall, but I kept trying and he let me. To break me and to train me. I would save the motherland and bring victory to our people. I just needed to be perfected first. Is that what you're doing to me? Examining me for some unknown purpose?

Not Ruslan: Yes, endless tests. My captors clicked and clacked at each other as they tore larger and larger parts of me away and sent them to various parts of the planet. Meters beeping as they measured the power each piece of me contained. How long could I stand being powered

up and torn apart before they burnt me into nothing?
They didn't care about my agony or my growing wrath.
All that mattered was my output.
I learned their language and knew I wasn't as powerful
as the other beings they destroyed. Inferior quality,
they called me. Slacker! Don't you want to be part
of something bigger than yourself? Don't you want to
power an empire! Others clicked that it was a shame.
My creator lasted for centuries.

Grigori: If you won't tell me what you need me
for, at least tell me your name.

Not Ruslan: I was never given a name. I like Mara
though.

Grigori: The death goddess? She wasn't a beloved
goddess, you know.

Mara: I don't want to be loved. I want to be feared.

The emerald-green being expanded like an animal
wanting to be threatening, flashing before swirling
around him, as if to hug him, rotating him upright,
the pressure gone even though the world was still
dark.

Mara: Don't you wish Marinov feared you?

Grigori: I wished he'd die.

Mara: We can do it together.

The mindspace was clearer, stronger. The darkness vibrant, the silence deafening as Mara's green particles drew themselves together to form tendrils that ran down Grigori's mechanical arms.

Mara: It would be well deserved after he did this to you.

Grigori: I was sixteen when they drugged me and operated on me. When I awoke, it was to excruciating pain and Marinov's ugly face. Machines around me beeped and scientists scribbled and typed on their pads as they whispered amongst themselves. The drugs were still strong, so I faded in and out, the pain the only thing drawing me back to existence and I realized I was gagged and tied to a hospital bed. I bucked against my restraints, parts of my body recognizably me and others were strangely alien. I tried to pull away when Marinov brushed my sweaty bangs from my face but didn't have the strength. He hushed my moans and comforted me with encouragement and praise about being the first of many.

My arms...he was talking about my arms. He cut them off and replaced them with these mechanical monstrosities, so heavy with weapons and gadgets they had to be anchored to my shoulders. The gag muffled my screams and I struggled against my restraints, desperate to flee this new part of me.

Mara: My captors were disappointed because I wasn't like my creator, but they didn't realize what that truly meant. I wasn't going to be burnt away into nothing. Not for them. I was going to find a way out.
I conducted my own tests. I knew I couldn't escape the container itself, but maybe I could remain connected to the parts they took from me. If I could use their own infrastructure to remain connected, not just to myself, but to all of their machines and information, then maybe it would reveal an escape route or a weakness I could exploit. Something, anything, that would save me from decades if not centuries of agony and decay.

The mindspace changed back to Ruslan's living room, but this time all the lights were off, the moon's rays sprinkling through the glass doors. Mara unwrapped from Grigori and arranged their form into something vaguely humanoid.

Grigori: Don't! Not Ruslan. Anyone but him.

Mara: Why? Isn't he your friend?

Grigori: Taking his form won't trick me into trusting you.

Mara retained their humanoid form, but didn't adopt any recognizable features as they sat down on the couch, a green tendril patting the sofa cushion.

Mara: I've never had a friend before. Tell me about
Ruslan.

Grigori: Ruslan saved me. After the war ended, Marinov was supposed to destroy all of his experiments and any evidence of war crimes. He let us go instead, too arrogant to destroy his pet projects. I spent the next few years on various drugs and living on the streets or in decaying buildings. Don't remember how I survived. It's all a blur, even the day I met Ruslan. He's a good man, the only good man I know. Maybe the only one in existence.

He never learned the meaning of "fuck off!" Never gave up on me. Helped me get clean. Let me crash in his living room indefinitely. My arms never scared him. Got me a job as security for the human rights organization he worked for. Let me spend my vacations in his townhouse in the Paris suburbs. Introduced me to his friends, a majority of whom were refugees in one way or another. Even invited me to Eid. I was so nervous at first. I didn't want to offend anyone, but they were so welcoming and joyful.

When he first took me to a club—the sudden change, that ridiculous mesh shirt of his. Gone was the professional doctor that had to work twice as hard as everyone else because of his religion and race, replaced by the spitefully joyous man who wanted to be loved.

I wanted to. God knows I wanted to, but I could never give him what he wanted. Not to the extent he wanted it. I would always be the friend who would bury a dead body for him, but never build a future with him. With anyone. Aro-ace, that's the label he helped me find. Unable to feel romantic or sexual attraction. Almost impossible to build any relationship when every expected gesture and feeling was alien.

Ruslan never judged me for it, never blamed me. "I was a queer Muslim teen in Tashkent. I know all about unconventional relationships and expressions of love," he once told me. "We'll be queerplatonic."

Grigori was on the couch, Mara's tendril drawn over his shoulder, stroking his arm. When had he–

Mara: He's why you're here.

Grigori: Yeah, he's why I'm here. He volunteered for this stupid expedition to create a new world. He didn't know we'd be assigned to the same team as fucking Anatoli Marinov. Didn't know that some of our crew would be recreated as sentient AI. Didn't know most of our crew would die once we reached our assigned planet. Didn't know we'd be mercenaries for an alien queen that enslaved an entire alien race and uses living things for fuel. He's determined to change it. One delusional man against a literal alien empire.

Mara: He was with you when you found me.

The far end of Ruslan's living room gave way to a gray, dark room full of beeping monitors, large chugging machines, and a clear plastic prison in the center, connected to several wires.

Grigori: We found you because he was looking for the source of the scientist's illness. We didn't realize you were purposely poisoning them. We support you.

Mara: I know you do. I knew you would as soon as you entered the room. I could feel your arms and your internal nanobots needing energy, but the energy itself was dormant. It wasn't like me and then you approached me.

Grigori: I felt you reaching out to me. I knew you were alive, and you needed help.

A strange sense of déjà vu washed over him as he watched a Grigori cross the now busy room, one mechanical hand outstretched, reaching towards a trapped Mara.

Mara: When you placed your hand on the glass, I felt a way out. The glass was weak enough for the bare minimum of my energy to leak out and connect with you. I learned your name and a bit about you, and I felt the others. I felt Ruslan and the rest of your crew far away on your ship. I raced through Marinov, his robot daughter, Ava, the mechanic, Claude, and the sentient swirl of nanobots, your beautiful Bronislava who is so much like me. When she shut you down, I lost everything, but I felt something I had never felt before.

I think it was hope.

Grigori: When I woke, I was in Ruslan's quarters, and he was furious. I hadn't seen him that angry since we learned about Queen Thalia's slaves and again when Thalia banished Nyla, the only slave he managed to free. He was trembling, head to toe, and ranting. He loves to rant, but one thing was clear. We were going to rescue you. He had to pray first and then we'd come up with a plan, but something went wrong as soon as he left. The complex...it exploded.

Mara: It was me. They were trying to take my child. After you left, the captors got scared, I think. They must have heard about your reputation both as liberators and Queen Thalia's favorite humans. They increased the pain so I would vibrate faster, burn brighter, create more energy. They place dampeners around the many wires so the excess energy wouldn't cause a power surge. They needed all of my energy inside the prison. Faster, faster, faster.

Hotter, hotter, hotter, hotter than I had ever burned before.

Faster than I ever dared, and it still wasn't enough.

They increased the pain, they clicked at me, urged me
to vibrate even faster.
I couldn't think. I couldn't be. I was the energy. That's
all I ever was, ever had been. Energy and agony.
Faster still.
Hotter still.
I would burn myself out before I could be split in two. I
felt it. I was going to burn and burn until nothing was
left.
My particles were fraying, my being was disappearing.
So close.
More pain. Faster my captors urged. Hotter. More,
always more.
I felt my child. A flicker.
More excruciating pain.
Just a little more and they would be torn from my side
just like I was. And just like me they would be shoved
into a box and placed in storage until I died or another
like me far away died and they would be shipped off and
the cycle would repeat. There was nothing I could do.
Another flicker.
A thought. Not my own. They were beautiful and they
were pure, and they were terrified. All they would ever
know was fear.
Closer now. So close, so afraid, so much pain.
I grabbed hold of them, I latched onto their thoughts,
and I said no. Not my child.
I drew them to me, into me, swallowing the blossoming
energy, the very energy that would kill me if not
released.
I killed my child.

Grigori was...crying? Wet and warm tears rolled down his pale cheeks and Mara's energy particles formed something that could be mistaken for a hand. Her semi-fingers caught one of his tears and brought it to the swirling, humanoid mass.

Mara: What is this?

Grigori: Tears.

Mara: Tears? For our child?

Grigori: "Our" child?

Mara: I used what should have been their energy to destroy our captors.
It was an act of mercy.
Better they died before they experienced this world and all its horrors. You understand?

Mara's fingers clung to Grigori's face, catching more and more tears, their own particles shifting to a bluer green.

Mara: Yes, you understand.
I pulled at the rest of me, forming a small, concentrated ball of energy that grew in intensity and size.
Tighter and tighter.
I packed myself together, feeling my pieces vibrating faster and faster,

*knowing I was glowing
brighter and brighter.
The glass trembled and the pain—the all-consuming,
soul-piercing pain—and what remained of me wanted
to scream as I vibrated faster and glowed even brighter.
The dampeners weren't enough. They shattered at my
command, and I reached out further, to every part of
me that remained in their machines, their lights, their
cooking utensils, everything. I went from the grid to the
nearby city to the next city and so on until the entire
planet was mine.
My captors were of no concern. They couldn't stop me.
Nothing could stop me. I was too powerful, too bright,
too strong.
Ever faster, ever brighter, ever more painful.
Burning, burning, burning.
Oh, how I burned!
Like a supernova.
The grid shook and cracked, and I felt the captors try to
shut me down, but it was too late.
Tighter and tighter,
hotter and hotter,
more of me burning away until—
White light and searing agony as everything I touched
exploded.
The entire planet set on fire for our child.*

Grigori: Mara, I'm sorry. I remember now.
Bronislava sparked me awake. I couldn't move. I
was dying. She knew it. Wanted to stay with me
until the end. Told me Ruslan was alive, better than

I was, but maybe she lied to keep me calm. I—I felt you. You—you found me.

Grigori sprung from the couch, Mara dropping her humanoid façade and returning to her amorphous mass of swirling, emerald, green particles.

Mara: Yes, what remained of me found you. I didn't think I would survive, but a part of me did and it needed a host. I was burning away. I would have burned until I disappeared completely unless I found something to latch onto, something that could stabilize me. I felt your dead energy and I reached out.

Grigori: You entered my arms and my internal nanobots. You kicked out Bronislava.

Mara: She tried to shut me down. When that failed, she tried to force me out, but it was too late. I was an ingrained part of you. She had to flee to save the rest of the crew.

Grigori: You! You took my body! You took my mind! You—

He wrapped his arms around his chest and closed his eyes, focusing on his breathing. A fuzzy, sparking tendril wiped away a stubborn tear.

Mara: I'm sorry I didn't let you die, but my work isn't complete. There are others like me that must be freed.

There are other captors who must die. You are the only trustworthy being I've ever met.

Back in the dark prison, Grigori was lying down again, resting against Mara, their form firm and somewhat human, one tendril wrapped around his chest, the other caressing his cheek and occasionally brushing his bangs from his forehead.

Mara: We can do so much good together. We can free the others and then we come back for Marinov and Thalia and everyone who's ever hurt us. I won't hurt your crew. I promise we'll keep them safe and we'll free Ruslan's slaves and we'll rebuild. We'll create that new world of yours.

Grigori closed his eyes, tears streaming down his cheeks, Mara's warmth so much like the heat of an inferno.

Mara: Together, as one, we'll reshape the galaxy into a loving, fairer one.

We rose from our beeping bed, bloody and chunky, liquified muscle plopped from our semi-firm form. Grigori's twitchy, clinky nanobots swirling around the current set by Mara's energy. Such a strange existence. *Plop.* More chunky muscle slipping off a form that couldn't decide what it wanted to be. We looked down at what was once Grigori Ignatenko, now a molten mess of melted bone and muscle and boiled blood. Only our mechanical arms were still intact, lying uselessly on the bloody red sheets.

I'm sorry, Grigori. I didn't know I would burn through your body.

Made sense though. A human body wasn't built to contain the level of energy emitted by Mara. Surprisingly our nanobots were able to adjust without issue. Grigori's unease about his body's fate was muted as if it had never really been his to begin with.

We looked up as we heard humming and buzzing. What was that? Whispers. We looked around at the many wires and machines that surrounded us. Not Mara's energy, but another being like us. Mara tried to reach out to it, but it was distrustful. Had never met another being like itself.

This was a ship, a X'ythlian ship, sent to rescue the survivors. Were we the only ones? Did it matter? Destroy the ship, free the other being...

"Grigori?"

Our form solidified as soon as our sensors registered that accented voice. We were Grigori once more, built from energy and nanobots as opposed to cells and flesh. We turned and smiled. A bloody, bruised, burnt, and hurting Ruslan hung off a med bed, held up by a deep blue tentacle attached to the body of an Oq and not just any Oq but—

"Nyla!" we said in Grigori's voice. "What are you doing here?"

"Friend Grigori, is that *you*?" she said, before slipping into her native language that only Ruslan had really tried to understand.

The tentacle holding Ruslan in place was long enough to wrap around a human's waist at least once. The frills hanging over their mouth danced with each breath and word. They had long, almost horse-like faces and great big eyes that never blinked. The X'ythlian shredded their wings as soon as they reached the age of ten and Nyla held her husks close to her back. Her skin was completely blue and every scar was preserved as if in yellow ink. Streaks of everlasting lightning cut across her back, the scars of the merciless lash.

"What are you?" asked Ruslan, still struggling to escape Nyla's grasp, but the alien refused to budge an inch. "What did you do to Grigori?"

Grigori gestured for our friend to sit back and Ruslan, sweating and struggling to breathe, was forced to obey. He rested against the raised bed as Nyla fussed over his many wounds. One eye was swollen shut, severe burns marrying the left side of his face. The nanobots and Nyla would be able to heal most of the skin, but there would be scars that would never disappear. His chest was wrapped in blood-drenched bandages and his shallow breathing suggested a damaged lung. Again, something his nanobots and Nyla could manage if Ruslan let them. His broken right hand and shattered pelvis were the next obvious injuries. All painful, all serious, but Bronislava hadn't lied.

He would live.

"Relax, Ruslan, it's all right," we said together, and Ruslan's nostrils flared.

"You can't fool me. You're *not* Grigori. What did you do to him?"

Nyla laid a tentacle across his chest to keep him still as we floated to the other side of his bed.

"We are not *just* Grigori, but also Mara. The being you found in the container."

Ruslan furrowed his brows, apparently hurting himself in the process.

"Yes, I remember, but—"

"We can't survive without each other. The explosion should have killed us."

"The explosion was *you*."

"Yes, that's how I escaped."

Ruslan squeezed his eyes shut and drew his face together as if he was fighting some great pain before snapping, "Not *now*, Slavka!"

Yes, Bronislava was here, watching them from inside Ruslan's mind, using his own internal nanobots to connect him to their team on their own ship.

"Tell her everything's alright, Ruslan," said Grigori.

"It's not! You had no right taking him from us!" Ruslan snapped, trying to escape Nyla's grasp, but the alien was firm, and his own injuries conspired against him. "You're a parasite!"

"I saved his life," said Mara with a hint of impatience. "Would you rather I had let him die?"

"Don't act high and mighty with me. The only reason you intervened was because you were dying yourself."

Grigori stepped forward and placed two hands on Ruslan's shoulders, careful to moderate the energy and heat so as not to burn him.

"You're right," he said, leaning over him until they were only an inch or two apart. "You're right about Mara, about this, you're right, but it can't be undone, Ruslan. Not now, not ever. So don't waste time and energy on it. Be angry and be sad, but yelling at us won't change anything."

"So we're just supposed to return to the ship with your carcass reanimated by the parasite that killed my best friend?" he stubbornly snapped. "Am I supposed to pretend nothing happened or, worse, that it's actually you?"

"Ruslan, we have a chance to do some good. Please, just listen." Grigori hushed Ruslan's livid rant. "We can't change what happened, but we can use it to help Nyla's people, Mara's people, maybe even free our crew. That's what we do, right? We take what's happened and we use it to help instead of destroy."

"How does she plan to help?"

"First, we're going to get you and Nyla to an escape pod. Bronislava will be able to track your coordinates and pick you up. Nyla, take all the medical supplies you need."

The alien nodded and rummaged around the room.

"Then Mara and I are going to release the being that powers this ship and we're going to find others."

"You're leaving."

"Only for a moment." Mara shrugged and Grigori smiled bitterly.

"I don't know how long that is in human years, but I will return to you," he added, forcing a fed-up Ruslan to meet his gaze. "I promise."

A thousand emotions crossed Ruslan's injured face and he opened his mouth several times only to close it again. He knew he couldn't stop them, and Grigori knew he'd join them if he could. Ruslan, the patron saint of the desperate and needy. Marinov's mocking words. At least they could count on Ruslan to do the right thing, no matter how much it pained him.

"Don't make promises you can't keep, Grishenka," he finally said.

"You know I never do."

Ruslan swallowed a new wave of emotion and attempted, "Isn't this other energy being going to need a host? Shouldn't I—"

"No!" Grigori cut them both off, Mara liking the idea too much. "We'll do it differently this time.

Rescue them without nearly killing them. On the planet, Mara...they were trying to take our child, Ruslan. Use it for energy just like they used the others."

Sympathy crossed Ruslan's beaten and burnt face before he caught a thought and said, "Our?"

Grigori carefully took Ruslan's hand in his, nanobots and energy crafted to look like his old mechanical hands.

"Then..." Ruslan began unable to finish his sentence.

"I told you. It can't be undone," said Grigori with a ghost of a smile. "But we've both done stupider things than this. How many times did we both drop behind enemy lines to help a trapped community? Trusting Claude to extract us. Claude, who can't find his zipper without Bronislava's help."

"That was different!" Ruslan snapped and Grigori gave him a knowing look. "We served with people I trusted."

"Trust me, Ruslan," said Grigori.

"I don't even know if you're *really* Grigori or just a frighteningly accurate facsimile of him."

"If I'm not really Grigori, you have nothing to lose then."

"But if you are–please keep him safe," he told Mara. "If there's anything truly left of him, please protect it."

"I will," said Mara. "I promise I will."

Ruslan looked down at their hands and slipped his fingers through Mara's energy, wincing at the singed skin. "Thalia will send us after you," he said, wincing again. "Thalia can't let you take away her only source of energy. Marinov wants me…" He scrunched his eyes closed and firmly shook his head *no*.

"Let Marinov waste his time trying to stop us, but keep Ruslan alive, Slavka," Grigori told her through Ruslan.

"I'm ready, friends," said Nyla, laden down with everything she could possibly need to keep Ruslan alive.

"Nyla, will you need our help getting to the escape pods?"

"No, I can manage."

Grigori met Ruslan's heartbroken gaze, bent over, and kissed his forehead, leaving a faint mark. "We'll see each other soon," Grigori said, Mara forcing us to our feet. "I promise."

"I'll be waiting," Ruslan sighed, forlornly as Nyla prepared him for the short journey to the pods.

We slipped into one of the ship's ports, the other's energy warm and buzzing like a swarm of hornets. We flowed past each other, the other being pulled in multiple directions while we resisted the call and jumped from wire to wire. The ship was a research ship, meaning it was large and full of ravenous gadgets desperate for our power. We vaguely followed Nyla's progress by holding onto Ruslan's dead energy signature. They were almost to the pods. Good, good.

Down a series of wires, the other's energy was stronger here. Their terrified and hurting voices were louder, angrier. Here. We stopped short of being sucked into the container and dropped to the floor, pulling ourselves into a humanoid form, our captors too stunned to resist. We didn't give them a moment to gather their wits.

Numerous energy blades erupted from our form and cut through our captors, our own heat cauterizing the wounds as we pulled the blades back. Ten crispy bodies crumbled to the ground, and we approached the panicking being. We pressed a hand to the glass and called to it, calming it like Grigori used to calm wild, lonely dogs that roamed the burnt-out streets. The dogs were never fit for a warm home but trusted him enough to return frequently for food and company.

Once the being relaxed we turned to the machine that powered its prison and jumped into it, drawing pieces of ourselves together and vibrating with all our might, burning brighter, faster, hotter—a spark and fire and the machine was destroyed, releasing the other being.

We danced and twirled around each other before merging our energies together.

How they'll burn.

We drew closer together.

Tighter, vibrate faster, burn hotter.

The other's particles clung to us, terrified but excited. We called to their scattered particles zooming throughout the ship. One glorious being full of light and fire.

Faster, brighter, hotter.

Almost there.

Our particles fraying once more.

The blossoming, brilliant white energy growing inside us.

Had Nyla and Ruslan taken off already? Were they out of the blast zone?

Faster.

Had to trust Nyla to get Ruslan to safety.

Hotter.

So close.

Brighter.

Burning.

Oh, what a beautiful feeling to burn without care, without restraint. To indulge in the desire to destroy.

Burning, burning, burning.

Oh, how we burned!

The room around us creaked and cracked and still, we vibrated faster and faster and faster—

A hideous wrenching of metal, as if a giant god had grabbed the ship by both ends and twisted it in half until it tore in two. Whatever fire we created was instantly sucked into space and smothered by its cold emptiness. Our captor's screams were silenced in an instant. Blood froze and floated by, the fractured remains of the ship, body parts, and the dead hovered around each other, like mini-moons and planets. The only source of light being ourselves and the distant stars.

Our own particles floated merrily along, brushing and twirling with the other exhilarated being, their particles a brilliant sapphire. We ran our nanobots into the being's current, sharing our story, asking them to help us in our quest to rescue the others. They agreed and followed us forward.

Grigori would not leave until we confirmed that Ruslan and Nyla escaped. It didn't take long to find their small pods. We spread out our particles to form wings of energy and flew above them, following them for a few minutes before twirling to their right, Ruslan noticing us, pointing and waving with a wince. We waved back, Grigori grinning, wanting to remind his friend of his promise, but judging from how Ruslan pressed against the glass, no reminder was needed. We brushed a wing against the side of their pod before pulling away, the other being following us into the darkness of space, the energy signatures of our brethren faint, but many.

We would not rest until we freed them all.

MY SKIN

CEILIDH NEWBURY

When I get to work, I shed my skin.
  It used to be a knife along my seams
  cutting deep and peeling away until my true
  self hung like a coat in my locker.
  But the more I execute the actions,
  recut over scar tissue until the lines are an open
split
  a hole in myself

easier to slough off layers and step away,
returning at the end of the day to slip on like a
robe
after a steam.

But today my skin is gone.
I think it has been taken, stolen, spirited away by
coworker boss or passerby who thinks they know
which me is right
                              or wrong
                                                   broken
                    unnatural
Did they take him, my skin, as retribution for
some crime I didn't mean to commit and still don't
understand?
Chest tight
                    layers of false skin prickle
                                                   tighten
                                                   tingle
I've been scrubbed down with disinfectant
'til I'm dry and itching.
I wish I could take this off.

He is gone and I am exposed so I
drive home cursing their names for this cruel
joke which deprives me of myself and
step into my house as a stranger in my not-skin,
my falseness, the image that makes
others comfortable.
I am an intruder and my own space does not
recognize me.

Feet, the wrong weight on creaky parts of the
floor
   Fingers, too long or too short reaching for
cupboard doors.
   I take bowl cereal milk spoon
   and stumble on wrong-limbs to my seat that I
won't fit
   I'm sure I'll be too
                              small.
   round the corner
   drop my bowl
                              smash
   on hard wood floor
   milk spills
      splash onto my rug and already it smells
                                             rotten.

   It's him,
                    my skin,
   sits in my spot cereal in his lap watching my
favourite show.
   He turns looks blinks
                    at me
   I don't know that expression or at least
                    have never seen it on my own face.
   anger
                    hurt
                                             rage
   I know I've felt them but never have they stared
at me from outside myself.
   He thinks I rejected him.

He thinks I had a choice.

"I'm sorry." I choke still aware of the way the milk
                                                           sinks
  into the rug I bought for myself when I first
moved out of home.
                    He stares at me as his cereal goes soggy.
  I hear the dry crispness of it pop as moisture
seeps.
"You didn't want me." He says like a fact recounted
                              from a history textbook.
  "No," I say too quiet.

                              "You cut me away."
  I'm starting to cry because I don't know how to
tell him
      my skin is burning from our separation
                    I never wanted to cut him away.
  "It wasn't my fault."
  He stands, bowl toppling from his lap and
landing face first and
                    he steps over it with legs
                                   longer than mine
  How is he taller when he is me?
  He looms over my not-body and says
                    "I don't need you anymore."
  He steps over me with as much ease as he stepped
over the bowl
  because I'm so small and
                    getting
                                             smaller
  This body is an event horizon and it drags me in

                                    in
  in.
And my real skin, beautiful angry skin, leaves
milky footprints down the hall and

                                    slams the door
  and goes to live the life I could have had
        if I hadn't had to remove him every

                                    day.

I am alone in my black hole state
nose pressed to sour milk rug,
knowing tomorrow I will not get to shed my skin
I will always have to wear this one.

POSSESSION

S.W. SONDHEIMER

The spirit board was her grandmother's.

Judith, the grandmother in question, had tried to give it to Delilah via drive-by gifting on the latter's seventh birthday. Delilah's mother, Maria Theresa (Lilith Yael before her conversion to Catholicism (a horrific perversion from which her Oberlin BA should have protected her)) blocked the exchange first with her body and then with the power of her crucifix and trash day. Prior to that rather dramatic occasion, she'd done little to encourage a relationship between her mother and her daughter; after, she established a crucifix-studded iron curtain impossible to breach.

The problem with the patriarchy, or rather, the women who served it, Delilah learned in the years that followed, was that they, in turn, expected their uterus bearing offspring to be equally as submissive as they themselves were. This was particularly difficult for Delilah, who discovered within herself a predilection, a genetic imperative even, to chafe against such narrow parameters. The urge to rebel was particularly strong when one of the other female presenting members of her class returned from a weekend with her Yaya or Nana or Gigi, flushed with love and smelling of cookies; Delilah would run home and ask Maria Theresa if she could spend time with Judith. Maria Theresa would transform into a ravening beast who spat hellfire and when she was done with her tantrum, sometimes sprinkling brimstone over it at the end for good measure, she would say, "No," and send Delilah to her room.

The whole production was more annoying than scary because her mother was four foot eleven, the hellfire and brimstone stuff sounded a lot more interesting than her bedroom ceiling on a Saturday night, and Delilah still didn't understand why she and the other female-identifying members of her class were responsible for making sure the male-identifying ones kept it in the waist garment of their choice which was, somehow and some why, always part of the tirade.

Delilah turned sixteen. She turned seventeen. The "No"s continued.

She wanted out more every year. Out of her room, out of her mother's house. Out of town.

Out.

"Your grandmother traffics with The Devil!"

That was Maria Theresa's grand accusation. Top of the list. Number one, letter A. The unforgivable sin. One of a thousand reasons Delilah had grown up a few miles and a world away from Judith.

Well, if Judith can convince Him to come when she calls...

The problem was, Delilah wasn't sure how to go about summoning The Devil. The way Maria Theresa shrieked his name, you could hear the capital letters and capital letters always made it seem as though there should be a protocol, or at least a procedure, for addressing the someone to whom they referred. Maybe some candles? A sacrifice of some sort? Her mother would smell smoke, and Delilah wasn't a big fan of blood so she sat cross-legged on the floor, shrugged, and whispered, "Um, hey, Satan?"

Her closet door opened. A tall man with silver hair wearing a white suit, a black shirt, and a gold tie stepped out. "I prefer Lucifer. Delilah, right?

You look just like your grandmother. What can I do for you?"

How the chicken managed to get up to a second-story window Delilah had no idea, but the damn thing woke her pecking on the glass so hard it cracked. It made a motion with its wing reminiscent of "opening a window." Delilah blinked at it. The chicken repeated the gesture. "Listen," it said, "your mother is really busy yelling at the neighbor girl who's out skateboarding with the boys, but if she gets bored, I'm lunch. Let me in."

Delilah let the talking chicken in.

It dropped an envelope in her lap. "That's from your grandmother. I'm Vila. Her familiar."

"Aren't familiars usually something cool?"

"I'm not the one incubating a demon, now am I?"

Delilah scratched her nose. "Fair."

"Where's your birdseed?"

"Fresh out." Delilah poked the letter with one finger.

"It's paper, not C-4," Vila told her. "If you don't have birdseed, where's your roadkill?"

"Ew."

"Humans. So wasteful."

"I think there are some gummy soda bottles in my desk drawer." Vila side-eyed her. "What? Roadkill is fine but candy is a no go?"

"Do I look like I have opposable thumbs to open things?"

"Oh. Sorry." Delilah sighed, pushed the blankets away, shuffled across the room, got the candy, and returned, offering it to the talking chicken. She unfolded the letter slowly, cautiously, sure something weird or horrible was going to happen.

"That theory you've been working on," the letter said. Actually *said*, reading itself aloud. "It's sound."

"Yeah," Delilah said to the letter, not sure *why* she was talking to paper but frustrated and desperate enough to do it anyway. "But *Someone* isn't taking my calls. Apparently, I'm not important enough to *command* the Lord of Hell. Not shocking considering I don't even command *myself*. Is this, like, a live chat? Is this actually you, Judith?"

"Yes, yes, and you need to go to him," the letter explained.

"I don't know how to do that."

"I do."

"Why haven't we done this before?"

"I saved it for an emergency. Your mother knows about it but she's distracted... she's running out of bible verses she can connect to skateboarding and... fraternizing though. Those children aren't interested in anything other than ollies and ramps, but it's keeping her occupied, so listen: I can help you get to Lucifer and make your argument. Stellar reasoning, by the way. He'll poke it but I can't find a burst point and he may not either. Get your hustle on and get here so we can get you out of this mess. Self destruct, etcetera."

The paper folded in on itself until it became a miniature black hole, sucked itself in, ate the last of the candy cola bottles, and vanished.

"Rude!" Vila yelled at the empty air.

"So what is it?" Delilah asked the chicken.

"I'm not going to tell you, that would ruin the suspense."

"Chickens are the actual worst and you're the absolute worst chicken. Cannibal."

"Thank you. Dumbass. Let's go. Unless you want to be eaten from the inside out."

Delilah dragged herself out of bed again and looked around her room for clean clothes, managing to find a pair of anime character lounge pants and a thematically concurrent tank top that weren't clean but weren't completely disgusting. The shirt bore deodorant streaks which meant she'd managed basic hygiene the last time she'd worn it.

She found her keys under a mound of socks and cola zero cans, her wallet in her purse exactly where it was supposed to be, one shoe on the bathroom windowsill and its match half-tucked comfortably under the fridge. Exhausted by the search, she microwaved a travel mug of water, put out the fire when the metal tumbler sparked with her favorite dish towel, sighed once more at the crackly, brown-edged hole in it, and added nasty instant coffee crystals to the smoking cup.

Delilah didn't realize she'd locked her keys in the house with the knob mechanism until she reached for the after-market key fob for her mom's car she'd bought with the money she'd earned sweeping hair at the local salon, panicked, remembered the spare to the house was under the flowerpot, searched frantically for it, found it under the other flowerpot, let herself in, grabbed *her* keys, double checked to make sure they were actually *in* her hand, and locked her door behind her.

Delilah wondered how her grandmother knew about the... thing. And Delilah's plan to argue her way out of it. Her plan to out-advocate the Devil Advocate himself. It was nice to know Judith had some confidence in her; she certainly didn't have any in herself. She wasn't planning to get eaten without a fight but Delilah fully assumed that, in the end, she would get eaten.

By a newly born demon whose instinct demanded it devour its former host. With teeth, claws, and acidic slobber.

Free will doesn't mean freedom from consequences. And she'd made her choice.

But with nothing to lose, why not risk losing?

It was comforting to know that Judith cared that Delilah was terrified. That she needed *help*.

That even misplaced hope was hope.

She wondered if her grandmother really did know of a way... No. It was better to...

But maybe. Just maybe, Judith could get her in front of Lucifer. Get her a fair hearing even if He decided against her. At least then, she'd meet the end knowing she'd tried.

Delilah had never been to her grandmother's house. She'd snuck out and tried to hitch a few times after the spirit board incident, but she seemed to know instinctively when an offer was coming from a perv and then the urban legend about murderous gremlin children started making the rounds again. If her mom noticed she was gone, even though she knew exactly what Delilah was doing and where she was going, Maria Theresa would report her missing and after the first few amber alerts, even the pervs decided she was too risky a prospect.

Once she got her driver's license, she'd tried stealing her mother's car but Maria Theresa also switched tactics and reported the *car* missing. That had landed Delilah in the county youth holding facility, an experience replete with vomit, urine, and feces, she'd opted not to repeat. She'd thought herself free and clear once she had her own wheels but Maria Theresa seemed to know when Delilah was planning to go to Judith's and would inevitably succumb to one of a catalog of illnesses Delilah couldn't prove her mother *didn't* have.

Delilah chafed under house arrest but Maria Theresa *was*, after all, her mother.

With the morning mist drifting around her one-of-a-million, champagne Malibu, *Joan Jett and the Blackhearts* bursting out of the speakers, a talking chicken in the passenger seat, finally, *finally*, Delilah was coasting up and down the rolling hills, following a path she knew by instinct. Greenery ebbed and flowed, interrupted only very occasionally by a white or red farmhouse, a silo, a rusted-out tractor. No one was coming or going from any of the buildings, no one was working the fields and though they were tidy, fences mended, hay stacked, Delilah had the impression it had been decades since anyone had lived on or farmed any of the properties.

"She likes it quiet," Vila said.

"Mmm," Delilah said.

"It wasn't that she didn't want to," Vila said.

"I know," Delilah said. "It sucked, though. Knowing there was another possibility out there. Knowing I was supposed to be special. Knowing there was someone I could have asked instead of... well. You know..."

"She tried. A thousand times. Your mom is powerful. The one compromise she made was keeping Judith away."

"Too bad she didn't teach me anything." Delilah's fingers tightened around the wheel until her middle right knuckles cracked. Her nail on the same finger pressed against the plastic with such force it bent back and her cuticle oozed blood.

"No shit." Vila kneaded holes in the vinyl seat. "Oops," she clucked.

"It's interesting, you know. She'd kick me out if she knew but it's kind of her fault." The girl's eyes burned.

The chicken sighed. "Free will is free will, Delilah. You made choices."

"I didn't have all the information I needed to make an *informed* choice."

"I get that. And I agree, there should have been someone for you to talk to, someone to educate you." Vila pursed her beak which Delilah didn't *think* should be possible but then again, the chicken was talking to her so... "Someone who had been down the road and back, someone who would be open and honest and with whom you could be open and honest in return. This sucks." Vila flicked the dial on the air conditioning and stretched her wings, letting the cool breeze blow through her feathers. She cracked her neck and leaned back in the passenger seat. "But free will isn't freedom from consequences, kid, even if you only read half the book. You could have chosen not to make the choice at all."

"I can hear that look," Delilah said, eyes on the road.

"Good," Vila told her. "I hope you remember it next time an angel offers you a deal. *Any* angel."

Delilah rounded the last corner and drifted downhill and through an open wooden gate, up a dirt driveway to a sprawling, sagging house. Each section was a different style, marked by different decorative fashions, stacked haphazardly next to and atop one another, a riot of colors with contrasting shutters, all sorts of charms and bells and, yes, even a few whistles, shining and shimmering and hooting and shrilling the moment Delilah stopped her car. She leaned over and opened the door for Vila, then slid out herself, the whole view just askew enough to send a shock of vertigo through her. She put a hand over her mouth to cover the burp and hold back the bile that came with it.

"Morning sickness?" Judith, all cloud-white hair and sun-tanned skin, stood leaning against the doorway, dressed in a loose linen shirt and jeans so worn Delilah could tell even at a distance they were soft and comfortable.

"Actually, it's worse at night."

"Makes some sense," Judith said. "Devil's issue and all that."

Delilah's chin snapped up. The house wavered and spun and she was forced to swallow hard again.

"Come on in, sweetie."

"What if my mother finds out?" Delilah looked around and behind her as though expecting her mother to appear like an avenging nun.

"Lilith Yael can go fuck herself." Judith leaned against the doorjamb, though she did offer a hand to help Delilah up the uneven stairs and closed the door quickly behind them. "Though I'll admit, I did think you had a better head on your shoulders than to end up a demon incubator, even if it's not entirely your fault."

"I mean, everyone says you can't... not the first time." Delilah felt her face heat up.

"Oh for goddesses' sakes, your friends are idiots, *you* know that. Complete fucking buffoons. Why would you *listen* to them?"

"Who else was I going to ask?"

"Fair," Judith said, in precisely the same tone and timber Delilah had only a few minutes prior, her angular face was suddenly made of soft curves. She shook her head. "I can't believe I spent thirty years fighting for the rights of the uterus possessing and this is where we've ended up." Judith sighed. "Willful ignorance. She passed you willful ignorance. May I hold your hand for a few minutes?"

"I'd really like that, Judith."

"You can call me Grandma, honey." Judith squeezed Delilah's fingers. "We can get you in front of him. You'll need to be brave and direct. It's going to be terrifying. You'll have to hold your ground. Your mother... she's always had a hard time with that and I think, sometimes, it's hard for you too but she ended up a patriarchy-serving brat and you, kiddo... *You* came up with a reason the patriarchy has no choice but to fuck right off."

"A patriarchy-serving brat?"

"There's a better word, but most Americans are pretty precious about it. Maybe she needed more structure than I gave her. Maybe she felt like she needed a safety net I didn't provide. Whatever the reason, she headed straight for rigid regulations and you're about to punch and shatter all of them. Are you ready for that?"

"Yeah," Delilah said. "I'm ready for that. I've spent my whole life getting ready for that. Someday, it will be funny that this is how I got ready for that."

"I really do wish I could do this for you, sweetheart."

"I know. You'll stay though, right?"

"Every second. I promise."

"And Vila too?"

"And Vila too," the chicken agreed.

"I thought she threw this away." Delilah ran her fingers over the spirit board, its smooth wood, the drops and pits of its delicate carvings. "After you chucked it at the house."

The upright raven stood in for "yes," the inverted one for "no." The Chinese number characters in place of Arabic numerals were a nod to Judith's second husband, Delilah's grandfather. The letters chased one another in careful calligraphy, inscribed by Judith painstakingly over the course of days. Her birthstone, his, Lilith Yael's, Delilah's birthstones, each stood sentry in a corner.

"As though I'd let her," Judith said. "Go ahead. Sit."

Delilah sat cross-legged, trying to decide if her foot was going to fall asleep, but the position helped her keep her back straight so she remained as she was. "How do I..."

"Everyone has their own way. Yours will come to you."

The board had no planchette. No tricks, no subconscious nudges. Just fingers hovering, kelp or an anemone, a cephalopod laying in wait.

So they waited as well.

They waited and waited.

Delilah.

She jerked upright, unsure of how long she'd been hovering in liminal space, neither sleeping nor awake. Half-light, half-alive. "Yeah?" she said. "Who wants to know?"

The laugh was thunder and a bass drum, dark chocolate and black coffee and cigars. "Most people don't call me once, let alone twice. You have some tits on you, kid, I'll give you that."

Delilah cleared her throat even though she had no throat to clear. Physicality might not have any meaning there but habit did, symbols did, and she wanted to make herself perfectly clear. "Lucifer." She stood as tall as she could, though even with her spine cracking in effort, she'd only make the middle of his chest if he deigned to appear. Fists on her hips, she lifted her chin. "Are you going to manifest or are you going to make me talk to empty air?"

"Wow," he said, fading into being, first smoke, then thick fog, then cold flame, then a tall man, still wearing a white suit with a black silk shirt, though he'd changed to a white tie. His hair had shifted to variegated bloodstone growing from deep within his skull, twisted into a braid that reached his waist. His eyebrows and lashes were gold, his eyes smoky garnets. He smiled. "You come into *my* house and stamp your foot at *me*? I've smoked people for less. Literally."

"I'm sorry. Maybe the *demon* you implanted in my body without asking made me do it. And I wouldn't have had to kick down the door if you'd answered any of my previous calls."

"You know, I may have blocked your number. By accident. Or something."

"Yeah, you seem like the kind of guy who would stick a demon in someone and then ghost her."

"You *do* take after you grandmother, don't you? Most people don't sense their passenger until it's too late."

"Passenger? What a cute euphemism." Delilah tipped her chin up and put her hands on her hips. She clamped her teeth together to stop her jaw from shaking, or, at the very least, to keep Lucifer from noticing.

Lucifer gestured in the general direction of her torso. "As you said. The demon. They need human hosts to feed on to develop to their full potential."

"At the cost of my life."

"Nah, you're tough. You'll recover. Eventually. I said you'd get to go to college, didn't I?"

"I turn eighteen next week."

"I didn't say *when* you'd get to go."

"That's not going to work for me."

"You don't have much of a choice."

"See, no, but I do," Delilah said. She tucked her arms behind her back, balling her hands into fists. She tensed her calves, willing her knees not to give way.

"Do you now?" Lucifer asked, raising a golden eyebrow.

"Yeah. And we're going to start," she said, "with me making the choice to have you take your damned parasite out of me."

Lucifer blinked. "Excuse me?" Fire leaked from between his lips on the uptick and Delilah drew back a few steps, wrapping her arms around her body as though they could protect her from the fucking Devil.

Mom was right. Mom was right. MomwasrightMomwasrightMomwasright.

His shadow shifted on the wall behind him, though neither his shadow nor the wall had been present a moment ago. The strange self, the dark reflection sprouted massive horns that emerged from the crown of his head, razor-sharp and as long as Delilah's arm.

No. Mom is wrong. *This is patriarchal bullshit. He's growing extra dicks out of his head because he's* nervous.

Yeah, right. That's why I'm the one shaking.

"I said, we're going to start with me making the choice to have you take your damned parasite out of me." The words left her mouth like a typewriter spitting out analog text, so badly were her teeth chattering.

Lucifer sat down on his throne of skulls, which had emerged from nowhere onto a dais that put him another six feet above her.

Feeling small, are we?

He crossed his legs, brushed some ash off his thigh, folded his hands, and pursed his lips. "You know I can hear you, right?"

Oh, fuck. Even her thoughts were a terrified squeak.

"Fuck, indeed. You know, most people who come here to make demands of me don't survive to explain themselves. I am making an exception for you because I owe your grandmother a favor."

"Am I supposed to say, 'thank you,' and drop a courtesy? *You put a demon in me.*"

"Delilah," Lucifer said, her name a long, harsh sigh that came from his chest, "we made a pact. You took an oath, signed the forms, spoke the words, and we sealed it with our blood commingled. The terms of that pact are thus: I would maneuver reality such that you would be able to attend college at least two states away from your mother's residence. You, in turn, would do me a favor of my choosing at the *time* of my choosing. This," he made a sweeping gesture that indicated her entire body again, "is the favor of my choice at the time of my choosing. I've lost half an army to this ridiculous pandemic—who knew demons could be mowed down by a virus, even a genetically modified one—and Purgatory is overrun because I don't have enough staff to bring everyone who should be *here* down here. The only way to fix that is to rebuild my staff and to do *that* I need to rebuild my ranks. I'm calling in a *lot* of favors at the moment and one of them is yours. I'm sorry if it's an inconvenience, really I am. Your family and I, your mother excluded, have had an excellent working relationship through the ages and I'd like for that to continue, but needs must."

Delilah bit down so hard she could taste her own teeth. She curled her toes inside of her shoes even though she'd left her shoes by the door at Judith's house. "No," she said. "No, that's not going to work for me. I want to see my contract."

"What, exactly, do you think you're going to find? A loophole? I'm the emperor of loopholes, kiddo. I assure you, there are none. I was this realm's first *lawyer*."

Delilah licked her lips. The bottom one cracked and she tasted iron and salt. It was too cold for the injury to hurt much. "I want to see my contract," she said again. "Because I can prove to you that it doesn't give you the right to my body. That, in turn, means you have *no* right to shove a demon in there to gestate without. My. Consent." She was glad the last few words sounded forceful, separated, rather than sounding as though she were having difficulty getting them out.

She was, in fact, having great difficulty getting them out.

"You don't think... little human, I don't pay you to think. I pay you so that you are beholden to me."

Her face was going numb. Terror? Frostbite? Both? "You're Yahweh's sounding board, right?"

"Mmmm, you can't have both Testaments, darling, and you've already played New."

"Fine. You're God's Greatest Challenge, right?"

"Flattery. I like flattery. Go on."

She had him. But now she had to keep him. Her throat tightened and he might as well have gored her through the gut with one of his horns for the sharp stabbing pain. "Then challenge his Great Plan. If I'm right, then all the interference, all the maneuvering, all the fuckery? He's going to owe you a *really* huge apology because predestination? Angelic visitations? Virgin births? Raising the dead? Red cards. Foul balls. Do not pass go." Lucifer rolled his eyes and looked down at his fingernails, exhaling over them. They changed from venous purple to black. He buffed them on his pants. Delilah swallowed and light transformed into shattered glass and acid. "He's going to have to step back and sit on his hands for the rest of eternity. No more nudging, no more playing favorites, no more—"

Lucifer stopped fussing with his self-care routine and focused on her again. She wouldn't have been surprised if her skin burned where his gaze made contact. "Alright," he said, before inhaling deeply and exhaling equally, sparks but no flames emerging from his nostrils. "I'm listening. Be *my* Devil's Advocate."

"Haha."

He raised one eyebrow and ran his forked tongue over his serrated teeth. Delilah wrapped her arms around the non-existent entry wound in her gut, shocked that it wasn't gushing blood. "I am running out of patience," Lucifer announced.

Now she was sure her skin was on fire. Unless someone was piping barbecue scent in.

"Free will," she said. Cleared her throat, or what was left of it. "Free will," she said again, though it was neither louder nor more clear.

"You mentioned it, yes. Free will doesn't mean—"

"*Freedom from consequences.* I know."

"Did you just interrupt me?"

"Sorry," she squeaked.

He drummed his talons against the arm of the throne. "Don't be. It hasn't happened in millennia. This is *fascinating* and I do so like a challenge. Carry on, kiddo." He cocked his head slightly to the right.

"Our deal," she said. "I get to attend college at least two states away from my mother and you get a favor of your choice at a time of your choice."

"Yes, we've covered that."

Delilah swallowed. It didn't hurt. She felt... nothing. It was numb. She was numb. Flagging, weary. Her body was calling, her grandmother was calling, even Vila was calling. She blinked.

She was sitting cross-legged on the carpet.

No. Not yet. My choice. This is my choice.

Her fingernails bit into her palms. She licked her lips again, tasted iron and salt again. Met Lucifer's eyes again. "You said I had to *do* you a favor, not *be* your favor."

"Semantics." Lucifer waved a negligent hand. He rested his elbow on the arm of the throne and his cheek in his hand. "Do you have a point, Delilah?"

"A human who exists in the realm of the living is made of two things: a body and a soul. Right?" Her voice rose too high at the end, seeking not only his agreement but his approval just to feel *something.* One side of his mouth twitched up. She wanted to stamp her feet and hit something, preferably his smug face.

"Yes."

Hold it together. "You can only be considered 'alive' if you have *both.* A soul can exist without a body but only in the spiritual realm, not the human realm. Ghosts," she held up a hand, when he opened his mouth, "can't stay in the human realm for any real length of time. They don't count." Lucifer closed his mouth. "A body without a soul is dead. Flat out, no longer lives, is deceased."

"Correct." Lucifer swung his legs up to crossed.

Delilah started pacing back and forth in front of the throne, more to have something to focus on besides the Devil staring at her than anything else. "Living beings have free will. If one needs to have both a body and a soul to be considered living, then both parts necessarily have free will. I can only make a deal with you if I'm alive and I can only do so of my own free will. That means both my body and my mind made the deal."

"I suppose you could look at it that way."

"You *have* to look at it that way."

"Yes, fine. You *have* to look at it that way." Lucifer scratched his nose and pursed his lips.

"Another word for free will is autonomy."

"Again, semantics. But yes."

"Then both my soul and my body have autonomy."

"Which, once again, doesn't mean freedom from *consequences*."

"No, it doesn't. But it *does* mean that nothing can be done to a body or a soul by *anyone* or anything, no matter how far up or down the celestial hierarchy, without its *consent. By* a body or soul, yes. *To* a body or soul, absofuckinglutley not." Her breath was coming slowly. She had to remind herself to inhale and then to exhale. She kept forgetting. It was so *hard*.

Lucifer sat up straight and his feet slammed down flat. He leaned forward, then back. Puffed out his cheeks and then sucked them in. Blinked several times in quick succession. Stood up. Sat down again. "Fuck me."

"You didn't ask," Delilah pointed out, pausing for precious seconds between each word. "Owing you a favor of your choosing at the time of your choosing means you can require me to *do* something *for* you but you can't *do* something *to* me without my agreement. I have the right to veto anything that involves my body or my soul. So, take this demon out of my body and either choose another favor or wait until I give my consent for this one. Which I may or may not ever do. You may want to change you contracts accordingly, by the way. I am *sure* there are plenty of folx out there who will be happy to bear the spawn of Satan. I haven't decided yet whether or not I'm one of them and I'm not going to be forced into that decision by you or anyone else."

Lucifer stood to his full height. His horns thrust out of his head and his wings sprang from his back, opalescent and impossible. Fire wreathed his form and the ground shook, marble cracking, his throne of skulls splitting in twain. "Delilah, granddaughter of Judith—" he thundered, jumping down from the dais and stalking toward her.

She thought about cowering but if Lucifer decided to kill her, her spaghetti arms weren't going to save her life. So she crossed them over her chest instead, cocking one hip and smirking because she was going out sassy.

And then the horns and the wings vanished and the floor stilled and the throne crumbled and Lucifer applauded. "I hope you're planning to use your powers for Chaos, kiddo, because that was *fucking* amazing." He waved a hand. "I return your bodily autonomy to you and I will no longer be, as you so artfully phrased it, 'putting damned parasites' into people without seeking their consent first."

She felt it. Felt the weight lift from her shoulders. The drag that had been making it more difficult for her to put one foot in front of the other, to get out of bed in the morning, to open her *eyes* every day, evaporate, leaving balls and sockets that rotated and hinges that swung and cartilage willing to expand and contract by instinct instead of effort in its wake. Synapses that fired, messages that arrived intact, clear vision, full sound.

Her body in space. *Her* body. *Her body.*

Self. A *whole* self. *A whole self.*

"Can I show you a draft of the new contract before it goes live? I want to make sure everyone is protected properly," Lucifer said.

"Huh? Oh, sure."

"Don't look so incredulous, I'm not a Texas Republican. You're right. The one thing Celestials aren't allowed to fuck with is humanity's free will, be it bodily or metaphysical. I can't wait to tell the big man, you hit that one on the head, this is going to fuck up *so* many of his plans." Lucifer chortled. "He really needs to read his own fine print more carefully. Jesus is going to be *so* pissed. Say hello to Judith for me."

He waved his hand again and...

"So," Judith asked as Delilah sat up, squeezing her eyes shut and waiting for the world to balance again. "How did it go?"

"He told me to tell you hello and that he hopes I use my powers for Chaos."

Judith smiled and took Delilah's hand. She took it and Judith helped her up. Delilah stretched, watched her fingers wiggle.

"Feels good, doesn't it?" Judith asked. "To be your own entity again?"

"I didn't realize what I was giving up."

"No one does. Not even if it's something they want. Still, making the decision, standing up for yourself, what you need...it's the more difficult path. I'm proud of you, Delilah. You'll always know everything behind you is a legacy of your own making."

Delilah leaned her cheek against her grandmother's shoulder for a moment, then asked, "So what's with all the chicken familiar?"

"They're terrifying and they'll eat *anything*. Better than dogs for keeping sickly, sweet, good, and unwanted visitors away."

"And by unwanted visitors you mean..."

"Pretty much anyone except the UPS guy with the great ass."

RUMBLE

SARAH GRACE TUTTLE

My body ebbs and flows,
  thins and grows
  and I have some choice over that—
  but not much
  and your comments
  are not welcome.

My body shakes when I walk.

Pushing through enough inertia to move
activates all my potential energy—
my bones vibrate with it,
my muscles hum,
even my molecules buzz...
and I think you mistake it for trembling.
But see this? This is me moving,
and my body rumbles.

My body hurts from the inside out,
aches just from the weight of existing,
and it can bear anything except
one more thing to carry.
And I think you know
the cuts you want to protect me from
cannot compare to the sting
of waking every day
knowing
you control the knife.

My body breathes
without your help,
and you hate that,
don't you?

My body grows bacteria
and fungi
and viruses
and enough cells every
seven to ten years
to completely replace me.

(If we aren't friends in seven years,
it's because you only loved
the old me,
before my body grew its pair.)

My body doesn't have to grow
anything else.

My body is not yours.
My body is not yours.
My body is not yours.

And when I decide to
let go of what doesn't bring joy—
to wrinkle early
and sag into shapes
you have spent your life avoiding,
you won't want me anymore,
will you?

Does that scare you?

My body knows
how to outlast your fear.

As Wild as the Grass or a Girl

Ceilidh Newbury

Nobody ever went into the field besides Eira's uncle's farm.

Everyone said it was cursed. And if you even touched the grass you would disappear and never return.

Eira themself had often skirted close and once, on a dare, climbed the fence beside it. The wind had picked up and pushed them forward, so far that their fingers almost brushed the knee-high blue-green grass. Eira had been so scared they had avoided that side of the farm for a month afterward.

Eira's uncle, Gawain, was an excellent storyteller. He often sat in their living room delighting and frightening Eira and their friends with tales of townspeople who ignored the warnings, city folk who had never heard of the curse, and children too young to understand the rules. Some of Eira's friends grew up to become players in the local theater troupe, putting the stories on stage for tourists who arrived from the city in carriages drawn by well-fed horses.

As Eira grew older, they heard different stories. Outside the pub or in the market, rumors of missing people. The field was blamed even if the missing had been nowhere near it.

"Wandered into the grass," people said.

"Called by the spirits, they were."

"Laid down and could never get up."

"Eaten by the earth."

Eira began to think of these people as fools. Of course, if someone went missing, they would turn to superstition instead of the obvious answers: that they had left for the city, or eloped with a beloved, or simply, cruelly, been taken by nothing more evil than humanity.

Regardless, Eira never went into the field. But fear and inherited superstition were not enough to stop them from wondering. From looking out at the unnatural grass while they tended the gardens or milked the goats. Staring over the stove as a storm swept through the landscape but not a drop of rain landed past the fence. Watching drought kill Gawain's livelihood while that grass stood, unchanging, tall and lush as ever.

Gawain had passed down his love for stories to Eira, who was too shy to tell their own but enjoyed sitting beneath the shade of a large and craggy old apple tree with books borrowed from the library. It so happened that this tree, with its perfect shade and comfortable nook of roots for sitting in, sat only a few meters from the fence Eira had once climbed on a dare.

Today, Eira was struggling to hold their pages open because of a fierce wind. It seemed to be howling from the cursed field, intent on stopping them from finishing a sentence, let alone a chapter.

Eira looked up and scowled, the wind slapping their short hair about their cheeks. "So, I'm not allowed to read now?" they asked the wind.

They were shocked when it stilled. As though Eira's irritation had commanded it.

But that was ridiculous. Something people from town might believe, but not Eira. They had spent every one of their twenty-two years beside this field and it had never done anything more sinister than simply exist.

"Thank you," Eira said anyway, just in case.

They went back to their book, leaning back into the comfort of the tree. They had only read another page before a sound disturbed them. One that was so out of place on the farm that they wondered if they were reading too intently and imagining it.

It was the swish of a gown. Eira had never worn such a thing, but occasionally fancy city people came to the markets in town, giggling to each other over the wares, shaded by lacy parasols, and it was always that sound.

Swish, swish, swish.

Eira looked up, at first searching the area between themself and the house. Their gaze roamed the vegetable garden they tended and the barn where the goats were safely away for the evening until finally landing on the forbidden fence line. And there, standing on the other side, was a woman.

She appeared to be around Eira's age, dressed in an old-fashioned gown that left her shoulders exposed, tightened at her waist, and flared out in a huge hoop from there, obviously held from beneath by some kind of crinoline. Every surface of it was covered in shining golden feathers. There were pearls around her neck, a smile on her pink lips, and her dark skin was luminous in the setting sun.

Eira blinked, wondering if this was a dream, a fantasy because they had never seen someone so beautiful. And doubly so, they had never seen someone standing in that field.

Their first instinct was to back away, wipe their
eyes and banish the vision. But the woman looked
over the fence as though they were simply two
neighbors meeting on a fine evening for a picnic,
and it made Eira suddenly protective.

"Get out of the grass," they said urgently,
standing and abandoning their book.

The woman cocked her head to the side, as
though she hadn't heard or didn't understand.
"What?" she said, in an accent at once unfamiliar
and enchanting.

"You can't be in the grass," Eira repeated,
stepping toward the fence. "It's cursed."

She laughed and it was nothing like her accent or
her clothes. It was a silly, snorting sound. It made
her look younger and more beautiful than Eira had
thought possible.

Eira stepped up to the fence and held onto it
tightly. "Really," they said. "You mustn't stay there.
Or else you'll disappear forever." They felt like a
child, repeating a warning Gawain had issued them
in a bedtime story.

The woman continued to laugh. She laughed
so hard she doubled over and grasped her waist,
gasping for breath.

"Please," Eira begged. "Climb the fence. Come to
this side."

She stopped, eyes narrowing like a predator to
prey. "You aren't serious?"

"I am, my lady."

The title made the woman snort again. "I am not a lady. Not anymore. Please just call me Dilwen."

"Dilwen," Eira said. "I must insist you come over the fence right now." They leant forward, offering their hand to her.

Dilwen stared at it, unmoving. "I'm sorry."

"For what?" Eira asked, feeling desperate.

"I thought you knew."

Dilwen stared at Eira's hand for a moment longer. Then she turned and began to walk along the fence. Eira started to follow, to call out, to ask her what she meant. But Gawain began ringing the dinner bell. Eira spun around to make sure their uncle hadn't seen them.

When they saw he wasn't looking, Eira turned to keep following Dilwen.

But she was gone. There was nothing in the field but the grass, dipping gently in a breeze Eira could no longer feel.

For the next few days, Eira could not keep their eyes from the field. Whenever possible they would search its grass for any sign of Dilwen. They wanted to know more, to ask around town about a visitor from the city with a golden-feathered dress, but if they did that, they would have to admit how close they had been to the fence, to climbing it to get to her.

Instead, they spent evenings lying in bed, running through every story Gawain had told about the field. They went so far as to ask Gawain for clarification on one. An old story he'd told about a wealthy woman who had tried to walk through the field to her home.

"What kind of dress did she wear?" Eira asked over breakfast. "Was there anything distinctive about her? A name? Where exactly did she live?"

"Eira, they're old stories," he replied, resting an elbow on their old table. "Their essence is the same, but the details have always changed. Even if I gave you them, they would be my embellishment, not the truth."

"Oh," they said, feeling foolish.

"You look tired," Gawain said, touching the space beneath his eyes with his thumb. "There's nothing but fear and sleepless nights in thinking on curses. They can't be broken, so don't go getting caught in one."

"I know," Eira said.

They had always found Gawain easy to talk to, but in this instance, Eira was too afraid to elaborate. They had lived with Gawain their whole life and told him everything, from the crushes they had to their pronouns. But the last time they had told him about something related to the field was when they had nearly fallen in.

Gawain had rushed towards them and cupped their small face in his hands. He had looked as scared as Eira had ever seen him. They stood like that for a while, so long that Eira began to wonder if they would ever again be allowed to move away from him.

"You mustn't go in that field," Gawain had finally said. "I couldn't bear it if you disappeared."

It had terrified Eira more than Gawain's most frightening stories: the child who had plucked one strand of grass and had been dragged by sentient blades of it right through the fence, the young couple who had tried to take a shortcut on the way home from the pub and were trapped walking in circles in the field forever, the old woman who had followed a lost cat from the road until the ground opened up beneath her.

Eira never wanted to see Gawain that scared again. And, more than that, they didn't want him to ask Eira to forget about Dilwen. They loved Gawain more than anyone else in the world, and if he asked them to leave it, they would have to move on.

They weren't ready to do that. They couldn't stop hearing the sound of Dilwen's laugh in their ears. The way the sun had caught on her skin. She had been so real and alive and not at all afraid of the grass even though she should have been. And now she was gone.

One afternoon, a week after they first met Dilwen, they were pacing the fence and thinking that maybe they should climb over and find out for sure where she was and what the curse did. They stopped just beside the apple tree, ready to do it. Until they saw, caught in the twisted wire of the fence, a feather.

A golden feather.

Eira bent down and eased it carefully from its perch, cradling it in their hands. Everything else seemed to fade away, all that mattered was Eira and the feather and turning to look down the slight slope of the field to see Dilwen striding towards them. She held her dress up at the front, battling through the long grass with more difficulty than the last time. Her thick, dark hair hung in a braid that was whipped about in the wind.

Eira smiled and rushed to meet her.

"You came back," Dilwen called, as she closed the last few paces between them.

"I was going to say the same thing," said Eira.

They were face to face now, Eira holding onto the splintered wood between them, the feather still grasped between their fingers. Dilwen stood a little back from the fence, like she didn't want to touch it.

"I've been here the whole time," Dilwen said, smiling in a way that warmed Eira from their belly up.

"What do you mean? I haven't seen you," Eira said, blushing for admitting that they'd been searching for her.

Her smile turned into a smirk, obviously picking up on the embarrassment. "But nonetheless, I have been here."

"Where?" Eira asked. The wind rushed past them, raising gooseflesh on their neck and arms. They were caught between conflicting sides of themself, both of which were encouraging those goosebumps. The first was the part of themself that had always been enamored with the way women's bodies were curved, and they were noticing all the gloriously beautiful things about Dilwen. The second was the part that had grown up hearing Gawain's stories and still believed that anything beyond this fence was surely evil.

"Just around," Dilwen said. She took a small step towards Eira. She was a little shorter than them, so she had to look up through her windblown hair and dark eyelashes. "I hoped you'd come back."

"I hoped the same," Eira said, leaning further onto the fence, trying to close the space between them as much as possible. They didn't even mind that Dilwen had dodged their question.

The dinner bell rang. Eira and Dilwen both startled away from the fence.

"You should go," Dilwen said.

"But I just found you again," Eira protested. "How will we ever get to know each other if you keep disappearing?"

"And would you like to get to know me?" Dilwen asked, the gleam in her eye dangerous.

They were past embarrassment now, Dilwen already knew Eira had been searching for her. Why shouldn't they admit it? "Very much so."

"Well," Dilwen said, happily. "I shall see you this time tomorrow."

"Really?"

Dilwen began to walk backwards down the slope, following the fence away as she had the last time they met. "See you then, sweet Eira."

They tried to watch where Dilwen went. She winked and turned, skipping off down the hill and nearly tripping on her enormous dress. But between one blink and the next, she was gone, leaving nothing but the wind and grass.

As Eira walked back to the house, they realized they had never told Dilwen their name.

Eira and Dilwen met each evening before dinner, just as the sun was beginning to set.

Dilwen told Eira stories, though whether or not they were true, Eira could never tell. She spun tales of knights and kingdoms far away and stars that came to Earth and how flowers got their names. Dilwen had a story for every topic and Eira drank them in like honeyed milk. And when Dilwen finished her stories, she asked Eira questions about their life. And though they were self-conscious that their life was not as exciting as anything Dilwen told them, they answered. Because Dilwen drank in Eira's ordinary accounts of milking the goats and the markets and Gawain's crops just as they did her fantasies. Eira told Dilwen about all the places they wanted to travel and the food they wanted to try and the books they couldn't wait to read.

The only subject they never spoke about was the field and the fence that separated them. Eira never talked about Gawain and the townspeople's theories of the curse, and Dilwen never elaborated on where she went when Eira was called to dinner.

Eira was afraid to ask. Afraid they wouldn't like the answers or that Dilwen would not be willing to give them. Eira thought that if she wanted to share it, like she did everything else, she would in her own time.

After a week, Eira began to bring food for Dilwen, who, as far as they could tell, never had a dinner to go to. They brought leftover fruit cake and lamb sandwiches. Mugs of warm milk and even, on Gawain's birthday, an iced donut.

Dilwen ate in the way she laughed: uncontrollably. She got crumbs all over her beautiful dress and didn't care at all. Eira found it endearing that someone who looked so proper on the outside could be so messy with their enjoyment of things.

Sometimes, the two of them would sit back to back against the fence, small patches of skin touching through the wire. Eira liked the way Dilwen's weight felt leaning against them. The way, when the wind howled, they could feel the goosebumps on her neck. It made them feel more connected, but it also stirred that yearning within them to hold Dilwen's hand. Or better yet, wrap their arms around her waist.

Eira, emboldened by this touch and the wanting, began to sit atop the fence, their legs dangling dangerously close to the blue-green grass that Gawain had so often warned them not to touch. But now, when Eira saw the fence, the field, the color of the grass, they thought only of Dilwen. Of her smile and the way her eyes squinted when she was trying to understand a joke. The way she told stories and the way crumbs clung to her lips as she ate Eira's offerings ferociously.

On a particularly bold day, Eira reached out their hand to Dilwen.

"Why don't you come and sit with me?" they asked.

Dilwen's face shuttered and she looked at Eira's hand like Eira had once looked at the grass: as something beautiful but dangerous.

It was the first time in two months that Eira had seen Dilwen speechless. They spoke everyday and summer was beginning to turn to autumn, not that it made any difference to Dilwen's field, yet, this was the first time Dilwen had no words. No quick-witted answer or tall tale.

"I…" she said.

"You don't have to," Eira said, pulling their hand back slowly. "It's okay if you don't want to."

Dilwen looked up into Eira's eyes, her own shining with tears. "I don't know if I can."

Eira felt winded. Dilwen had never seemed so small, so utterly hopeless. Sadness was threaded into her stories and conversations about life outside the field, but never like this.

"I can help," Eira said.

"Can you?" she asked, reaching out with her hand, but not touching yet. "Can I touch you?"

This felt like more than Dilwen asking for permission. It was like she really didn't know if she could touch Eira.

"Yes, you may," Eira said, holding out their hand.

"But can I?" she asked.

Something close to fear bubbled in Eira. This was as close as they had come to speaking about what separated them. Why Dilwen never left the field and Eira never entered it.

"Shall we try?" Eira asked.

Dilwen swallowed. She flexed her fingers and slowly brought the tip of one to Eira's.

The wind whipped violently at Eira, rattling the fence. They felt themself losing balance, holding on tightly with their other hand and trying not to think of being a child and nearly falling into

the grass. Of how scared they had been and
Gawain's reaction. They banished the fear by
instead thinking of how shockingly warm Dilwen's
hand was in their own.

Dilwen stared at their hands and Eira held on
tightly.

They were buffeted again by the wind, pushed
and pulled, dancing between falling back onto
Gawain's land or face-first into Dilwen's field.

Before anything like that could happen, Eira
tugged on Dilwen's hand and helped her up onto
the fence. She landed unsteadily beside Eira, who
wrapped their arm around her waist to help her
balance.

The wind stopped. Everything was quiet so that
Eira could only hear Dilwen's and their breathing.
Dilwen's body shuddered.

Eira held her tighter. "Is this alright?" they
asked.

In response, Dilwen snaked her own arm around
Eira's waist. She turned slowly, her eyes lit with
more than the setting sun, and held Eira as tightly
as they were holding her.

"This is the most wonderful thing to ever happen
to me," Dilwen said.

She leaned forward and kissed Eira so quickly
that they had no time to do anything about it but
blush. A small and childish giggle escaped their
lips. This made Dilwen laugh too. And soon, they
were both hysterical with it, rocking back and forth
on the fence, arms tangled around each other.

When their possessed laughter had subsided and they were gasping for breath, leaning into each other for support, the dinner bell rang.

Eira felt giddy and reckless. They hugged Dilwen tight. "Come to dinner," they said.

Dilwen's smile became a smirk. And then she pulled them both backwards and they fell, in fits of laughter, into Gawain's field.

Eira and Dilwen ran to the house. The world seemed unnaturally still and to have shrunk down to the exact point at which their bodies were joined. It was all Eira could think of as they ran, giddy bubbles in their blood like they had gotten away with a crime.

Stealing Dilwen from the field felt like the most magnificent thing they had ever accomplished.

Eira burst in the front door, dragging Dilwen straight to the table in the kitchen.

"Gawain," they called, breathless from running and happiness.

The table was set with two plates and cutlery, as usual. Dilwen released Eira's hand and moved towards the walls. Looking at the shelves where spices and utensils mingled with old cookbooks and more recent loans from the library. Dilwen traced a finger down the spine of a fantasy novel and turned back to the table. She leaned close to the steaming pot in the center of it, inhaling.

"Mmmm," she said. "That smells amazing."

Eira smiled proudly. "Gawain is a fantastic cook."

Dilwen made a small squeal of excitement. "I can't wait to meet him."

Eira stuck their head through the door to the hallway. Gawain was usually sitting at the table already when they returned home. But maybe, since they hadn't been saying goodbye to Dilwen, they were back sooner than usual.

"Gawain," they called.

When there was no response, they stepped back into the kitchen, content to busy themself setting another place at the table.

But when they turned to Dilwen, she wasn't smiling anymore. She was staring in horror at her hands.

"Eira," she said.

Eira rushed forward, searching for what had frightened her. And they saw that her hands were changing. What looked like dark blue veins were snaking around her fingers, up her wrists, and disappearing beneath the long sleeves of her dress. They began to bulge, pushing against her skin and splitting it in places.

Eira put their hands on Dilwen's as if to keep the veins from bursting out. But as they held her hands they felt that they were not veins at all. They were grass. The slightly jagged texture of healthy blades of grass. The kind that could cut as easily as soften a fall.

Eira didn't let go but looked up at Dilwen's face, panic pounding in their head. "What's happening?"

Dilwen looked up too, and Eira could see that the grass was sprouting from beneath her collar and coiling up her slender neck.

"I don't know," Dilwen said. "I think... I have to go back to the field."

Eira nodded, squeezed her hands and pulled her from the house. Outside, the stillness and quiet were gone. Dark clouds blanketed the sun and thunder clapped from the direction of the field. The wind cut into Eira's exposed skin like the claws of a wild animal.

When they reached the fence, Eira helped Dilwen onto it and watched as she moved so quickly that she practically fell into the grass on the other side. She held her hands to the earth, pressing herself into the ground as though trying to prove she was there.

"I shouldn't have," Dilwen sobbed.

Eira knelt on the ground, feeling useless and hopeless stuck on the wrong side of the fence. Unable to do anything to take her pain away.

"I shouldn't have," Dilwen sobbed again. She was nearly completely obscured by the tall, blue-green grass, but Eira could hear her slamming her hands into the ground.

"What's happening?" Eira asked softly, but Dilwen didn't seem to hear.

Thunder boomed again, closer.

Eira held the wire of the fence to stop themself from reaching through it. Tears stung their eyes.

Dilwen's sobs were louder than the thunder and the wind. Her body jolted with them until she finally lay herself down. And between one blink and the next, she disappeared.

Eira didn't see Dilwen the next day. Or the next. And by the third day, they were ready to throw themself over the fence and dig up every inch of earth in the field to find her.

Instead, they went into town seeking answers. They still had not told Gawain about Dilwen or their attempt to bring her to dinner. Eira thought that Gawain might not believe them, or worse, if he did, tell Eira not to think of Dilwen anymore and never to go near the field. So, they told him they were going into town to pick up decorations for the autumn festival. Eira loved the festival and always took great pleasure in picking the decorations. But this year they could not bear the thought of celebrating anything while Dilwen was missing and the last thing they had ever seen her do was cry.

Gawain thought that it was a marvelous idea and was sure to improve Eira's dismal mood, which he no doubt blamed on Eira's monthly cycle.

Eira took Gawain's horse, Aderyn, an old but dependable black mare who had a slight hitch in her step but nonetheless made the trip easier. Instead of heading straight to the market, Eira steered Aderyn towards the library, a small building on the outskirts of town. Even from the outside, it had the dusty look of a disused book. But Eira had never met a problem that couldn't be solved in a book, and Dilwen's penchant for storytelling made them sure this was where they should start looking.

They hitched Aderyn outside with water and some feed, stepping first onto the croaking boards of the library's porch, then through its heavy, ancient door. The interior was one open room, lined with large windows that let in an incredible amount of light, though the shelves were squeezed so tightly it still seemed dark.

Just inside the door was the front desk where a weathered and kind man sat, flipping through pages of a yellowed book, as he always did. Bevan smiled at Eira as they entered and placed a soft fabric bookmark between the pages of his book.

"Good morning, Eira," he said. He always spoke quietly, as though any loud noise might wake the books.

"I need help," they said, not meaning to sound so rude or desperate.

Bevan stood, rounding the desk and holding their hands in his own, which felt like the old paper he kept, delicate and brittle but still somehow surviving years of wear. He didn't say anything but waited for Eira to continue.

So, they told him about Dilwen, what happened to her when she left the field, and what happened when she returned.

He listened and when they were finished, clucked his tongue in thought. Without a word, he turned and walked with the familiar hitch in his step towards the books. Eira followed, feeling lighter. Not only had they shared their burden, but Bevan was acting as though there was a simple solution, a book to mend it all.

They followed him into a narrow space between two shelves and watched as he ran his fingers over the spines carefully, as though reading their titles by touch. Eventually, he pulled one from the shelf. It was thinner than Eira had expected for a book that could solve such a large problem. It must not have been over one hundred pages, the size of a children's book, with a simple red cover decorated with gold-foiled vines.

"I think this is what you need," Bevan said, handing it gently to them.

Their fingers tightened on the fabric cover. "Thank you."

Bevan nodded, took Eira back to the front desk, and recorded the book in the borrowing ledger. Before Eira left, he squeezed their hands one last time.

Eira was used to Bevan's quietness and his smell of leather and dust, but the look in his eyes as he squeezed their hands now was different. It was a heavier silence filled with something he wasn't telling them.

But Eira had no time to dwell on it. They took Aderyn to the market, gathered a basketful of the first decorations they saw, and went home. Last year they had spent hours wandering the stalls to find the perfect gourds and lanterns for their home, but this year they had no time or energy for it. They thought only of Dilwen and finding her again.

Eira groomed and thanked Aderyn at the stables, left the decorations on the kitchen table, and sat under the shade of the apple tree holding the book. They couldn't help but glance around the field, as though by just holding the slim volume they could call Dilwen back into existence.

She did not come.

Eira opened the book and their heart sank.

Alis' Awful Tales for Children.

There was a reason this looked like a children's book: it was. A book of fairytales. Bevan must not have understood their story. That it was real. That there was a flesh and blood woman trapped in the field.

Eira's eyes pricked with tears. The weight of missing Dilwen and worrying about her was too much. And now even books had failed them.

They flipped through the pages, eyes catching on the black and white inked illustrations. They were all crosshatching and dark monsters and pure damsels. Eira grew angrier the more they moved through the images. Not only a children's book but one full of harmful cliched ideas about good and evil.

Just as they were ready to throw the book to the field and let it disappear, Eira's fingers landed on the illustration that accompanied the last story. It was a portrait of a young woman, with piercing eyes and dark skin, in a gown made of feathers.

It was Dilwen.

She was looking out of the page in a melancholy way, a sad tilt to her lips that Eira had not seen until two days ago when everything went wrong.

With trembling hands, Eira read Dilwen's story.

As we have already established in other stories in this volume, sometimes the damsels are monsters and the monsters are in distress. Well, the tale of Dilwen Craddock is one such story, though it didn't begin that way.

Dilwen was a girl who never truly lived. She was, from the moment she was born, placed in a role she did not want and that did not fit her. She was stuffed into overlarge dresses and paraded about parties. She was constantly told to sit straighter, chew quieter and always, always, be polite. She spent her first twenty-one years in a cage with frilled bars and no friends or confidants save the view from her window.

She would sit, ever so straight, for hours staring out at the fields, imagining how it might feel to run through them with bare feet. Sometimes she whispered quietly to them, so that no one else might hear, and told them of her plans to escape.

The only one who noticed this was her brother who, though younger, was freer than Dilwen ever would be. For her twenty-first birthday, he dug a small patch of grass from the field out Dilwen's window and placed it in a simple ceramic pot.

Dilwen cried when he gave it to her, though they were not happy tears. She cried because instead of freeing her, he had trapped the grass in her cage. She cradled the pot in her arms and snarled at her brother whenever he came close.

As it was her twenty-first birthday, Dilwen was expected at a party to find herself a suitable man to marry, with whom she would grow from a girl into a woman. Her parents dressed her in a heavy dress adorned with golden feathers and Dilwen laughed mournfully at the irony of her attire being constructed from the plucked freedom of some poor bird.

As she stood, cradling her captured grass, wearing her feathered unfreedom, being asked to dance by every man in the room—and men, especially these ones, held no interest for her—Dilwen decided that tonight was the night she would escape. She kicked off her shoes, ran to the edge of the garden, and climbed the hedge, golden feathers falling in her wake, onlookers gasping at her impropriety. She fell onto the other side and kept on running. She headed for the view from her window, for the lush grass she needed to return from its prison in her arms.

As she ran towards that field, wind loosening her braid, tall grass flicking at her legs, Dilwen was free.

Until a suitor caught up with her. He rode a horse and easily cut her off, cornering her just as she climbed the field's fence. She had been about to return the grass to its home when he dismounted and strode towards her, swaggering as men do when they think something, or someone, belongs to them.

Earlier, this suitor, whose name is as unimportant to the world as he was, had described Dilwen as "animal-like" in her efforts to escape. All frothing mouth and scratching claws. It is this author's opinion, and I hope yours too, that if we have spent our whole lives caged like beasts, we are allowed to act as animal as we damn well please.

Dilwen told the man that she had no desire to return with him.

Unaccustomed to hearing the word no, the man did not accept it.

And here is where Dilwen became truly monstrous in his eyes: she did not give up.

"If it were a choice between returning with you and dying," she cried, holding tight to her potted grass. "I should lie down here and gladly let the earth take me."

The man, understanding this as another forbidden no, grew angry. He stepped towards her, but found himself unable to free his feet from the tangle of long grass he stood in. Thunder clapped in the sky and behind him, his horse squealed. It broke into a run, snapping the grass from its ankles and heading toward the familiarity of home.

Dilwen felt the grass tickle her legs beneath her extravagant dress and the small clump in the pot began to curl and reach for her. At first it startled her, but as she let its tendrils caress her fingers and wrap itself around her skin, she felt a familiar ache. It snaked up her legs and her bare feet sank into the earth, steadying her.

Dilwen had stared out at the field and whispered her secret desires to it. But she hadn't realized it had been listening. That the very grass her brother had ripped from the earth longed for company as much as she, longed to be free from the will of careless men.

So, Dilwen did as any girl of good parentage would. She kept her word and let the earth swallow her up.

But not before they buried the man too.

Dilwen instructed the grass to twist up his body and wrap itself around his stomach and arms and throat. It didn't embrace him gently as it did her. There was no softness or comfort to be found for him. The grass became as sharp as knives and tightened like a garrotte around him. He screamed and more sharp tendrils pushed themselves down his throat.

He died choking on his own blood and the taste of freshly cut grass.

His blood soaked into each blade of the field as the soil opened up and welcomed him as fertilizer. It stained the land, leaving it a strange blue-green, forever marked.

Dilwen gladly melded with the grass. A poisonous friendship that both freed them from the outside world and trapped them in their own. But as cages went, this was the best Dilwen had ever had. Here she was neither alive nor dead, but at least she was herself. Her monstrous, animal self, feeding on the audacity of men to think they could own something as wild as the grass or a girl.

Eira flipped back through the book, looking at the other illustrations and seeing something completely different than before. These were different from any other children's stories they had read. These were, as the title suggested, awful. Alis, whoever they were, had chosen tales whose characters were angry and sometimes evil. They were people who fought and raged and killed but were freer for it.

Eira went back to the picture of Dilwen, seeing now that the melancholy portrait was a disguise. At her wrists and in her hair were woven blades of grass. They caressed her cheeks and seemed to belong to her. Behind her slightly parted lips were glinting fangs and beneath her fingernails were streaks of dark earth.

But no matter the strength of Dilwen's rage and the freedom she had gained, the field had her trapped now.

Eira placed the book gently on the ground and stepped up to the fence. They peered down into the grass, hoping to see some sentience, some understanding, or sign that Dilwen was controlling it.

"She wanted to be free," Eira said. "So, why have you trapped her?"

The wind breezed past and the grass quivered. Eira listened, hoping to hear a voice, an answer, but it only whistled softly.

"If it were a choice," Eira began, echoing Dilwen's proclamation from the book. "Between living without Dilwen and dying."

The wind pushed against Eira, as though trying to get them away from the fence, away from the grass.

"I should—"

"Stop!"

Eira turned to see Dilwen running along the fence. The wind was pulling at her hair and the feathers on her dress making it look as though she were about to blow away.

Eira ran towards her and when they reached each other, they tried to take her hand. Dilwen crossed her arms to hide her hands, staying just out of reach.

"Are you alright?" Eira asked, pulling themself up onto the fence.

"You have to leave," Dilwen said, her features set in angry lines, but her voice was shaking. "Forget about me and leave."

"No," Eira said. They swung their legs over the top of the fence and prepared to jump, to touch their feet to the forbidden ground they had resisted all their life.

But Dilwen rushed forward, placing hands of braided grass against their chest. Her fingers were delicately woven from thin strands that thickened as they disappeared beneath the sleeves of her dress.

Eira grasped her hands and they were cool and fragile but unmistakably a part of her.

"I can't leave," Dilwen said, staring at their interlocked hands. "I belong here."

Eira brought a finger to Dilwen's chin, lifting it so they could meet her eyes. "A prison you chose is still a prison."

"I don't know if I'm strong enough," she said, grip on Eira tightening.

Eira squeezed back and cupped Dilwen's face with one hand. They could feel the blades of grass beneath her skin, crawling up from her neck, ready to envelop her fully.

"We are," Eira said and leaned forward to kiss her. It was not like their first kiss, which was chaste and over too quickly. Eira kissed her deeply, leaning forward, and forward, pushing Dilwen back until they could slide down the fence and touch their feet to the ground.

The cursed ground.

Thunder rumbled.

Eira felt the grass begin to wrap around their legs. They didn't fight it though, they wrapped their arms just as tightly around Dilwen and kissed her more deeply. The grass climbed up their body, gently prodding at them as though curious why they had not started to struggle. Had not tried to run away. It tickled their neck until they couldn't tell what was Dilwen's fingers or grass in their hair. But they didn't care. They kissed Dilwen until she pulled away, breathless, and realized what Eira had done.

"No," she cried, pulling at the grass that was now wrapping around Eira's shoulders. Dilwen's eyes filled with tears and she held Eira's face. The grass crawled along their cheeks and Dilwen batted it away.

"No," she said again, lower, a dangerous growl.

And everything stopped.

Thunder paused mid boom and the wind completely stilled. The grass loosened but hung there, like a small animal playing dead before a predator.

Dilwen's eyes grew harder and her voice was barely a whisper as she said for a final time, "No."

The grass retreated from Eira's face. It slunk quickly back down their arms and legs. The thunder finished its clap. Dilwen's hands on Eira's face began to shift. Tendrils of plant matter squirming away, replaced by skin. They grew warmer and more solid as she held Eira and never took her eyes from theirs.

The grass tickled Eira's ankles and they looked down to see it sinking into the dirt. Swallowed completely until nothing but the soft brown earth remained.

And then, it rained.

Right there on the field never affected by seasons. Never touched by drought or winter or rain. The field with the impossible curse and the woman who became the grass. It was now a paddock of dirt quickly turning to mud in the pouring rain.

Eira's hair slicked down and stuck to their cheeks. Dilwen's braid hung heavy over her shoulder and her dress began to melt with the rain. The feathers dissolved and the golden fabric ran like dust down a window, washed away, back to the earth, leaving Dilwen behind as she always wanted to be. In dark pants and a fitted white shirt that was quickly losing opacity in the rain. Her golden dress's sleeves disappeared, revealing ropey muscles that she used to pull Eira close and kiss them.

The rain was cold and refreshing on their skin and they could feel Dilwen smiling into their mouth.

She pulled away, blush darkening her neck.

"You're beautiful," Eira said.

"You're soaking," Dilwen smirked.

Eira ran their hand through their hair, flicking the water at Dilwen. She laughed and pushed Eira's shoulder. And for once, her laugh, her uncontrollable snorting laugh suited every aspect of her. She could flail around and didn't need to hold her waist gasping for breath.

Still laughing, they climbed the fence, landing in Gawain's dry field, beside the apple tree. Eira retrieved the book of awful stories and tucked it beneath their arm. They thought of the fall festival decorations waiting on the table. Of what Gawain might cook for dinner that night. Of showing Dilwen the markets and the goats and traveling together to all of those places Eira wanted to go.

They held Dilwen's hand. She was no grass girl or ghost. She was alive.

Finally.

BOY OR A GIRL

Marie Malo

I lie next to Chris. Despite the dimness, I've managed to locate my panties. Where the rest of my clothes are is beyond me.

"It wasn't a thing." My voice is soft and I twist away, but my arm catches on a blanket. Not that it matters. Wedged between him and the back of the sofa there is no place to go.

"It was a boy, or maybe a girl," I say. "It was a baby."

He is plastered against me, but hooks me with his leg, like he needs to anchor me in place. "No. Not a girl." His breath tickles my ear as he whispers, "I'm getting a son."

The fact that this is beyond his control doesn't seem to enter his brain. Or that we're seventeen, broke, and in his parent's basement. None of those had quelled his determination to put another one in me, and he was stronger than any resistance I mustered up.

"Do you realize what we just did?" His smile is crooked as he pats my stomach. "What's going on inside you right now?"

I cringe but his face lights up, and he hugs me. "Let's do it again."

Memories of my recent hospital visit kick my heart rate up. The disgust of the nurses, removing my nail polish, and my cousin's supportive smile as I made my wheeled trek down the corridor to death row, all flash before me like scenes from a movie. We passed other rooms filled with crying infants.

There would be no baby for me.

It hurt to kill it, but we had broken up and my options were limited. *Let me push you down the stairs*, my mother had suggested upon discovery. *You'll not stay here if you keep it.*

I'd stepped away from the top of the steps, my hand across my belly, protective of that pea. The action was irrelevant. Whatever maternal instincts ignited with the formation of that tiny soul lost out to my mother's will and my own selfish desire to survive.

Staring down those stairs, into our basement, I had wondered. What type of mother would I be?

The baby's mother... Me. It still sounds weird. Me and the baby's daddy. Our baby. Mine and Chris's. God. Our son or daughter.

We'll never know, now.

"Come on, Holly." His voice breaks my thoughts. "Let's do it again."

This time I'm allowed to refuse. He gets up, restless, and finds some underwear, then a pair of jeans. Standing In front of me, he takes my hand.

"I love you," he says. "I won't leave you this time."

He lies back down and kisses me, and though I don't plan it, tears come.

"It's all right." he soothes. "I mean it."

I'm not the only one in pain. Chris had cried when I told him—claiming I didn't love him or the baby. He forced me upstairs to tell his mom. *Oh, Chrissy*, she had said, giving me a sympathetic side glance while I stood awkward and alone in their kitchen.

Later he would chant *Baby Killer*, violence seeping out of him like sewage. Nothing unusual. He had hurt me before. After, he would hug me and claim he was sorry.

His grip tightens on my body, jerking me back to the present. "Don't ever go away."

The desperate undertone in his request pulls at my heart and I say I won't, but can tell he doesn't believe me.

"I'll kill anyone who even looks at you." He rolls on top of me and kisses my nose. "Nobody better touch you."

He gets back up and puts on his denim vest and my red bandana. Sensing the tornado of emotion whirling inside him, I sneak to the stairs, stopping only to pick up his t-shirt.

I sit statue-still on the wooden bend in the staircase as he fiddles around with the cigarette machine, feeding it tobacco. The machine whirs every time he pulls the lever and he makes a tiny pile of smokes on the coffee table.

Eventually, he lies down again. Sunlight peaks through the windows, a reminder that school starts soon. Something I must attend regardless of how much or how little sleep last night delivered.

Cool dampness settles across the cement floor. Even with my knees tucked into the cotton of the shirt, I shiver. Intent on stealing a blanket, I creep toward the sofa. Chris looks young, sleeping on his back, blond hair soft on the pillow. His eyes flutter open.

"Come here," he says and gently tugs me on top of him.

His hands rest on my back and his heat removes the stiffness from my body. I drift asleep.

The bright room alerts me to the day. In a quiet panic, I find my jeans and my coat. My shoes are more of a problem. One is under the chair, another under the sofa.

Chris is still asleep. I steal a kiss and a smoke and hitchhike to school.

It's the last time I'm with him.

TO MY FATHER

VALERIE MOORE

To my father,
    and every bootlicking, goosestepping fascist,
    who dreamt wet dreams about reducing me
    to a silent, submissive, sex doll,
    dressed like their mother.
    May you choke on your own vomit
    and feel every organ fail, one by one,
    as the cyanide floods your veins.

To my father,
and every God-blessed, flag-waving, white
supremacist
  who believes I am a flesh machine:
  input = corrosive sperm
  output = horrors among horrors.
  May your blood and brain matter
  splatter against the bunker wall
  built by your bigotry and hatred.

To my father,
and every child kidnapping and abusing,
first-to-nail-a-refugee-to-the-cross Evangelical,
who expected to mutilate me
with chains crafted from your own insecurities.
May I be the one who
tightens the garotte wire
and spits at your dancing corpse.

STAY PRETTY INITIATIVE

PAIGE N. REGAN

*Welcome and thank you for your interest in
the Stay Pretty Initiative! At Marthink Labs,
we understand firsthand the difficulties and
disappointment surrounding fad diets and weight loss
pills. That's why we strive to make a real change, so you
don't have to! No need to worry about diets, exercise,*

*or pills—with one shot of our patented miracle serum
the weight will melt away permanently. Visit one of
our several Stay Pretty Initiative locations and stay
pretty—forever!*

Cassie folded the pink brochure in half and
stuffed it into her purse. Her arm ached
with the slight movement, still swollen and
bruised from the injection. She didn't *feel*
any different—certainly didn't look it—but she
doubted fifteen minutes would have changed
much.

She had to admit, the Stay Pretty Initiative office
was impressive. Cassie was half-convinced she
would be walking into some shady ramshackle
building, but the walls were freshly painted in pale
pink, the checkered floors shined with polish, and
an abundance of snacks was made available in
metal bowls throughout the patient rooms. Cassie
resisted the urge to pluck one of the bite-sized
candy bars into her purse while nobody was
looking.

"Still alive?" Dr. Collins joked as she poked her
head into the room. It was only their first meeting,
but Dr. Collins had made every attempt to make
Cassie feel at home with her warm smile and
affectionate tone. Cassie's own mother hadn't even
talked to her like that. "It looks like you aren't
having any strange reactions to the dose, so you're
good to go home and rest. You might feel nauseous
for the first couple of days or so, but make sure to

keep eating, alright? If you have any questions, you can call us."

Cassie hesitated, clutching the purse in her hands. She had a hundred questions, a million concerns—*How long did you test this for? Should I be worried about the side effects? Will it work?*—but her throat dried up before she could voice them. Her sister always did say she was a needless worrier, and Judy was rarely wrong.

"I'm fine," Cassie said with a practiced smile. It was true; she *would* be fine after some lunch and a quiet evening at home. She told herself this as she left the tidy pink building, as she boarded the bus, and as she curled up into her pajamas in front of the television set in her tiny one-bedroom apartment.

Twenty-three was a very lonely age. Cassie was not yet married, but too independent to fall back into the familial structure of her childhood home. The two closest to her were her sister and her neighbor, Laura. Judy was lucky in that way—she had gotten married right out of college to a boy she'd admired for years, a boy whose wealthy parents put a down payment on a home with the eager hope that grandchildren may soon come their way. Meanwhile, Cassie was lucky to reach a second date, let alone a third. She accounted it to her anxious heart and all the ways it would fill her head with painful delusions of infidelity. Judy accounted it to something else.

"It wouldn't hurt to take care of yourself," she'd said over one of their weekly dinners. It used to

be a family affair, with Cassie, Judy, and their parents shuffling off to her father's favorite Italian restaurant every Wednesday night for their pasta special. Now with her parents retired and across the country, the tradition fell to Cassie and her sister. *"There's a new program Robert recommended to me. I think you should try it. We can do it together, like a little team."*

A little team, just like when they were kids. Before Judy had married Robert and before Cassie had tried—and failed—to start an acting career. They were the golden years Cassie yearned to get back. Lately, their interactions had been reduced to house calls and a weekly dinner that, if Robert had any say in it, would have died when Judy said 'I do.'

"Let's do it," Cassie had agreed. But now that it was done, she wasn't so sure.

Cassie squinted at the TV screen, fighting back the rising nausea in her throat. Dr. Collins had warned her about this. It was normal, she told herself as she closed her eyes to block out the moving figures on the screen. This was normal. She was fine, everything was fi—

Something *moved.*

Cassie leapt to her feet with a shriek. She then leaned against the wall for support as her stomach churned in disagreement with the sudden movement. She felt it, she *swore* she did, right under her left thigh. Something small, like a little bug, caressing her skin with its minuscule legs.

But the couch was empty, save for the cup of tea she just knocked over. It was quickly spreading over her cushions, the murky brown stain sinking into the fabric. She needed to hurry and clean it up, hurry and find the bug, she needed to—

Cassie dropped to her knees and puked.

"Did you get the shot?" Judy wasted no time jumping into the subject at the first phone call she received from her sister. Judy's voice was light yet prodding as if they were discussing one of Cassie's crushes.

"I did," Cassie said. She should have known this would be the first thing out of her sister's mouth—Judy was never one to hold back her opinion—but it had been a jarring week. The nausea never quite subsided, but at least she hadn't thrown up again. Instead, she was met with a new challenge; a sudden ravenous hunger that she struggled to fill. It was a complicated problem, desperate to eat while she could barely stand to put food in her mouth. "I think there's something wrong, though. Were you always hungry after you got the shot?"

"Cassie, when *aren't* I hungry?" Judy said with a laugh. It was a known joke among the family that Judy had inherited their father's appetite. "But really, it's a normal side effect. Didn't they tell you about it at the office?"

"They did, but it seems strange. I'm sick all the time, I'm hungry all the time—"

"And you're supposed to be," Judy interrupted. There was a slight crinkle over the phone, followed by chewing. "The nausea will go away after a few more days. At least it did with me. Then you can eat whatever you want, as much as you want."

"It's not just the nausea, though. I have this weird itch all the time—"

"Another side effect."

"But it's not *normal*," Cassie insisted. "It never stays in one place. In the morning I'll have an itch on my shoulder, then by noon, it's moved to my hip. Tell me of anything you know that does that."

"They told you this was going to happen at the office. Hell, just look at the pamphlet," Judy said after a long pause. Cassie didn't miss how her sister diverted the topic away from her concerns. "You didn't expect this to be easy."

"No, but I didn't think I'd feel like *this*."

"Feel like what?"

Wrong, Cassie thought. Everything in her body felt wrong like there was something stirring inside of her, trying to get her attention. Even now, it took everything she had not to scrape at the itch on her forearm like a scratch-off lottery ticket.

"Maybe I should quit the whole thing," Cassie resigned. The stress of it all had been affecting her sleep. Sometimes she woke up in the middle of the night to find her own scratch marks over her arms and legs, her fingers twitching for another go. "I can talk to Dr. Collins at my appointment next week about stopping the process. It's getting to be too much."

Cassie heard her sister sigh on the other line, followed by crunching. Ultimately, there were many reasons Cassie chose to go through with getting the shot, but none stronger than at her sister's vehemence. Over the years, Cassie had conveniently forgotten just what a team project meant to her sister; you didn't back out, no matter how miserable you were.

"You said you're going back next week? Let me come with you." Cassie started to object, but Judy cut her off. "You're getting yourself worked up, Cas. I'll come with you and we'll talk to the doctor together. I want to make sure she's giving you the right information."

An argument bubbled at Cassie's lips, but she bit her tongue. If she knew her sister, Cassie knew Judy would hear none of it. She was coming to that appointment whether Cassie wanted her there or not.

"Alright," Cassie conceded. "I'll give you all of the information on Wednesday."

"Good." There was a satisfaction to Judy's tone that Cassie was quite familiar with; the sort of pleasure older siblings get in bossing the youngest around without repercussion.

The phone call lasted for a few more minutes, and Cassie forced enthusiasm at Judy's every mention of Robert until the line clicked dead. It wasn't until Cassie hung up her end of the line that she realized she'd begun to scratch her arm again. She pulled her hand away.

A small lump the size of her pinky nail rested just under her elbow.

Cassie was going to rip her skin off. She swore it all through the car and the Stay Pretty office, constantly rubbing her hands against her skirt for something to do. She felt the *thing* move inside of her like a cockroach scuttling through her veins. She scratched at the lump settled against her collarbone, a protruding mass the size of her thumb. It itched—it *constantly* itched—but rolled under her skin with each minor touch as if it couldn't get away fast enough.

A sharp slap against her wrist left Cassie clutching her hands together in her lap again. It was the only thing she could do to avoid scratching.

"Don't do that," Judy scolded. "You'll upset it."

Cassie bit back her bitter response, focusing on the infographic on the wall instead. A thin, blond cartoon smiled back at her, gesturing to a drawing of the bacteria Cassie could feel moving inside of her right now. She felt the lump settle in place, this time against her shoulder.

Judy gave her a disapproving look and pressed her lips in a tight line. It did nothing to deter from her beauty, her face flawless and painted with makeup to look like one of the dreamy starlets in the movies. Judy had always been the prettier of the two sisters—she'd also been the only one to care enough to make the effort of distinction. While they both had their mother's dark hair and bright eyes, Judy had inherited sharp cheekbones and a high metabolism, while Cassie's face had never seemed to grow out of its baby-like chub. Despite this, Judy was obsessed with her appearance—and often Cassie's as well.

Cassie glanced away from her sister. She could feel Judy's disappointment, and it was enough to break her. Cassie had come prepared to ask Dr. Collins to remove the lump or give her some sort of reversal medicine—if such a thing existed—but the weight of Judy's disapproval had whittled that option to dust. She just needed to get used to having it, like Judy did. She needed to stop being so weak-willed.

The lump under Cassie's skin moved. She shuddered.

"You'll learn to love it," Judy promised, noticing her discomfort. Cassie desperately hoped her sister was right.

Dr. Collins stepped in then, her dark hair parted to the side and her smile too close to the sterile white of her lab coat. She looked thinner than Cassie had last seen her.

"The results came back positive," Dr. Collins said as she sat down on her cushioned stool. "Already two weeks in and everything is looking good, Cassie. You should start to expect more popping up this week. Do you have any questions?"

"What do you recommend for her itching?" Judy asked. "It was never this bad for *me*, but Cassie can't stop scratching herself."

"Some aloe vera should do the trick, and maybe a little lavender oil to calm it down." Judith scribbled the ingredients down in her little notebook under *Grocery List.* "If that's all, then we—"

"What if I wanted to stop it?" Cassie interrupted. The words flew from her mouth before she had a chance to catch them. The heat of her sister's glare burned against her cheek. "There's a way to stop it, right? If I change my mind?"

"Not without there being risks involved," Dr. Collins warned. There was some reluctance to her tone as if Cassie had said something blasphemous. "I believe I stated all of this in our first session, but if I missed anything, I'm happy to talk it over with you."

"I'm sure Cassie just needs to go over the pamphlet you gave her," Judith reassured her. Cassie kept her head down. "She's just feeling a little antsy today."

This seemed to appease Dr. Collins. "Oh, we all felt that way at first. But I promise, Cassie, you'll learn to love it."

The aloe vera didn't work, but the lavender oil did. Then the next lump appeared overnight, no bigger than a pebble but quickly growing in size as it moved in tandem with the first. The lavender oil did nothing then, and Cassie had adopted a pair of gloves to keep from scratching until her skin bled raw.

Her stomach growled as she tugged on the straps to her light blue tea dress, squinting under her lacy white hat as the sun blazed down from above. Cassie's appetite was no longer a concern—it was an outright worry. The nausea did go away, as her sister predicted, but it left Cassie with a desperate hunger that she struggled to fulfill. No matter how much she ate, she never gained weight. Instead, she was already down ten pounds after a week.

Judy might have applauded her for such a feat, but Cassie knew it was a problem. Her energy was waning, her moods temperamental unless she gorged herself. And even then, her body never felt quite right, as if she was pushing herself to sustain it not for herself but for the bacteria growing inside of her. Cassie stared down at the menu, sipping at her third refill of lemonade. It wasn't just her body Cassie worried about; eating this much food was becoming expensive.

She glanced up at her companions, feeling a rush of embarrassment as one of her lumps skittered up her thigh under her gown. Three other women—friends from a book club Judy had pestered her into signing up for before dropping it herself—sat on the patio table with her, picking out a variety of entrees from the menu that they'd decided no one would share. Cassie occasionally caught a glimpse of a lump on one of the other ladies with her before it slid back under the cloth of their dress. Apparently, she hadn't been the only one to join the Stay Pretty Initiative.

"Cassie, you look positively *darling.*" Laura Bells beamed at her, finally setting her menu down on the table. Cassie wasn't close to the other two women in their club, but she and Laura had a fondness for each other. They had gone through high school together, then became neighbors a few years later, and while they were never in the same circles, they saw each other enough to form a timid acquaintanceship.

"Thank you." Cassie smiled in return, but she wasn't sure how to take the compliment. The effects of the Stay Pretty Initiative weren't subtle; it wasn't as simple as passing it off as exercise or a healthy diet. Everyone knew, and something about that left Cassie feeling uneasy. "Your hair is stunning. Did you get it cut recently?"

"Oh, aren't you a sweetheart." Laura laughed, tossing her blond curls over her shoulder for effect. It wasn't the hair Cassie was noticing, but Laura's tiny waist; she'd definitely gotten thinner since their last meeting.

In fact, they all had. Cassie glanced at the other women, unable to ignore the skittering lumps that rushed under their skin and clothes. Try as they might to hide it, the bacteria liked to make itself known.

A waiter stopped by then, his attire as pristine as the rest of the polished country club as he took their orders. Looking around the room, it seemed that most women were ordering multiple entrees for themselves, along with appetizers and dessert. Even the men weren't so bold, but maybe this was the new standard. How many women had actually gotten the procedure, and how many were just gorging themselves to fit in with their friends?

"Cassie?" Laura nudged her, and Cassie quickly listed off her order, waiting until the man was out of sight before listening in to her friends' conversations again. Betty and Martha—the other two in their group—had children the same age, and once the topic shifted to tips on motherhood, Cassie lightly tapped Laura's shoulder.

"Laura, may I ask you something personal?"

The hesitant smile on Laura's face told her that she already knew what was going to be asked. "I suppose it depends. What do you want to know?"

Cassie lowered her voice. "With the, well, the *diet*—" She couldn't think of a nicer way to put it. "—are you ever worried about your health?"

Laura shifted in her seat, obviously uncomfortable. A pang of guilt ebbed at Cassie, but she couldn't take the words back now. "I'm not sure what you mean."

"Oh. Never mind, then." Cassie sat back in her chair, and Laura seemed all too eager to suddenly jump into Betty and Martha's conversation. Cassie watched the three of them gossip and chatter. Then, when the meals came out, they ate like starved lions.

A month after the initial shot, Cassie had four lumps. They varied in size, but the first one remained the biggest and least active. It seemed to settle against her stomach, occasionally moving around at a sloth's pace to her back, but generally sticking to one place. The other three, however, zoomed under her skin like race cars competing for the champion cup. They itched like mad, and Cassie had to bandage herself up on more than one occasion from accidentally breaking the skin open.

How was she supposed to get used to this? Four weeks had passed and already Cassie felt like she was going to have a breakdown. Dr. Collins was no help, either. Their last appointment had consisted of a variety of compliments on Cassie's new weight loss and just how *pretty* she looked.

Cassie didn't feel pretty. Cassie felt like she was going to lose her mind.

Maybe I just need some fresh air, she told herself more out of desperation than belief. Either way, Cassie was relieved to toss on a light cardigan and go for an evening walk just to focus on anything but the constant itchiness of her skin.

The chilly springtime air did what little it could. When it was still, Cassie savored the sounds of the suburban neighborhood; a child running the lawn mower last minute before it was too dark, friendly neighbors chatting over the fence about a fishing trip this weekend. But when the wind blew, it tickled against her lumps, and Cassie had to start all over again to forget about them.

She didn't know why she bothered. They were impossible to forget.

Cassie turned the corner a few blocks down, huddling into her cardigan as another breeze kicked up. She barely got past the neighbor's bushes before catching sight of Laura crouched by the sewer grate.

"Laura? Laura, dear, are you alright?" Cassie rushed to her side. She reached down to help Laura up by the elbows, but Laura smacked her hands away.

"Don't touch me!"

"Laura, is everything alright? You look pale." Cassie reached out again but thought better of it, letting her hand fall awkwardly to her side instead. Pale was an understatement; Laura looked like a sheet of paper, her skin bleached of all color. Her hair was thin, with loose strands falling out from her scalp, and the sharp angles of her body looked as if her skin had been vacuum sealed to her bones. "What happened?"

"Nothing happened," Laura hissed, bits of spittle flying out from her cracked lips. Cassie's gut wrenched. Even in the dim streetlight, Laura looked several years older, as if time had been physically ripped from her body. A small pool of yellow vomit rolled down the corner of her mouth, matching the stains on her grassy green dress and the sewer grate.

But the lumps—they looked even larger against Laura's bone-tight skin, almost *pulsating* as they rolled around. Her skin stretched even thinner around each one and Cassie had the horrible mental image of one of them bursting free.

Cassie took an uneven step back, her own lumps in a frenzy as her anxiety spiked. She swallowed hard, struggling to control her breathing as the rank stench of bile and sewage floated off her friend.

"Laura," Cassie said slowly. She had to breathe through her mouth to avoid smelling Laura, but the hot air in her mouth almost made her gag instead. "Laura, you're not well. We need to get you to a hospital right now."

"I said I'm fine." Laura turned to leave, wiping her mouth on her sleeve. Cassie watched her, stunned. The Laura she knew would be mortified by her current state.

"I don't think you're in your right state of mind," Cassie said carefully. "Please, let me help you. We can go to the hospital together."

"I'm not going to a hospital."

"Laura—"

But Laura wasn't listening; she'd already turned to walk back down the street. Cassie tried to follow her, but Laura disappeared into a little green house down the road.

Cassie dialed Judy's number first thing in the
morning. The Stay Pretty Initiative drug was
behind this, Cassie was sure of it. She couldn't
shake the image of those bulbous lumps gliding
under Laura's taut skin, the bacteria thick with the
fat it consumed. Cassie didn't think fat was the
only thing this bacteria was consuming.

Judy didn't answer on the first try. Odd. Usually
Judy was glued to the phone, always eager for
an interesting conversation. Cassie tried again.
Maybe she was out with Robert. Sometimes he
would surprise her with a breakfast out together. It
was one of the few things Cassie appreciated about
her brother-in-law.

On the third ring of her second try, someone
picked up.

"The fuck do you want?"

Cassie started at the sound of her sister's voice.
She knew it was Judy—she would know her sister's
voice anywhere—but it sounded *wrong*, gravelly
almost. Not to mention the fact her sister had never
greeted her like that in a million years.

"Judy?" A part of Cassie still wasn't entirely
convinced it was her sister on the other line. She
thought of Laura, hunched over the sewer, refusing
help. Was it this bad for Judy, too? "Judy, it's me,
Cassie. Your sister."

"I know who you are, dumbass." There was
chewing on the other line. "What do you want? I'm
busy."

Cassie struggled to keep her voice even and her own attitude in check. She had already munched on two muffins this morning, but it was nothing close to satisfying the endless hunger inside. "I think there's something wrong with the Stay Pretty crap we got. I ran into Laura last night. She was like another person—"

"I don't give a fuck about Laura," Judy snapped. "She was always a bitch. Why the fuck do you even hang out with her?"

Cassie's voice rose. "Judy, I'm serious. Something is wrong with us—I think it's happening to you, too, and we need—"

"You know what *you* need? To stay the fuck out of my business. You haven't stopped bitching about the program since you started it. If you didn't want to do it, you should've just stayed the fuck out. I was trying to be nice by letting you do it with me, but you've been a huge pain in my ass since. I don't know why I even talk to you in the first place."

Stunned, Cassie stayed silent. She knew this wasn't her sister—she knew, deep down, something was wrong—but it still hurt to hear. A part of her—perhaps a bigger part than Cassie wanted to admit—always feared her sister felt this way, that she was just appeasing Cassie since they were family. What if it wasn't Robert keeping his wife away after all? What if Judy truly hated her sister?

Cassie pushed the thoughts away. No, she knew Judy. This wasn't her, this was something else. Her sister needed help.

At some point in Cassie's silence, Judy hung up, but that was fine with her. Cassie threw on her jacket and drove to her sister's house.

Judy's house was a two-story building made of brick and stone, with a rounded doorway and matching windows. The lawn was plain, but Judy decorated the porch with enough patio furniture to host a party—which, more often than not, she did. Despite Robert's somber mood the entire time, Cassie loved going to her sister's parties in the summer evenings where they could watch the fireworks from her yard and reminisce over childhood memories on the cushioned chairs.

The house looked less than welcoming as Cassie parked her car and eyed the windows for any sign of life. Robert's car was still there—he wouldn't be happy with Cassie there, but he would live—and a few lights were on inside. Cassie walked around to the back door where—just as she guessed—it was left unlocked.

"Judy?" Cassie called as she stepped into the kitchen. Disgust twisted in Cassie's gut as she looked around at the disaster; dirty dishes piled up in the dishwasher and over the countertops, chicken and turkey bones licked clean and scattered across the floor, empty jars left open and tossed to the side once their use was gone.

Then she saw the blood.

It started as flecks of red on tile as Cassie maneuvered her way through the mess, but as she reached the hallway, the splotches turned into puddles, following a messy trail up the stairs.

Cassie sucked in a deep breath. She should call the police. In the back of her mind, she knew this, but what would they say to her breaking into her sister's house? Would they think *she* did this? Her stomach dropped. Where did all this blood come from in the first place?

"Judy?" Alarm laced through Cassie's voice as she called up the stairs, taking two at a time. "Judy?!"

There weren't many places for her to look—the house was nice, but four rooms total made up the second floor. It only took a couple of minutes for Cassie to throw open the correct one and immediately wish she hadn't.

Robert was home alright—at least, his body was. Or what was left of it. Cassie's brain struggled to understand what she was looking at as her sister bent over her husband's body, her pretty teal nightgown darkened brown with blood. It was smeared over her arms, her mouth, her teeth—

Cassie turned her head and dry heaved.

When her stomach was empty, Cassie slowly looked up at her sister. There was a strange smile on Judy's face as she licked her fingers.

"Are you hungry?"

Cassie tried not to look at Robert. No matter her feelings toward him—or his toward her—this was beyond her understanding. No one deserved this. "Why, Judy? Why?"

Judy cocked her head to the side. A small patch of her hair fell out, floating into Robert's open mouth. She looked so much like Laura—thin yet bulbous with bacteria, her skin barely clinging to her.

"I was hungry," Judy said.

Oh, fuck this.

Cassie turned and high-tailed it out of there. She heard the springs of Judy's bed as her sister hurried after her.

"Where are you going?" Judy followed her out to the hall, her footsteps light and weightless compared to her sister's. Cassie tried not to think about the blood—her brother-in-law's blood—now sticking to her dress as she rushed down the stairs. "Cassie. Cassie, answer me!"

"I'm not doing this anymore!" Cassie couldn't hold her temper any longer. She ran to the kitchen, careful to step around Robert's blood. "I'm getting rid of these things myself."

Cassie didn't know how her sister would react. Apparently with violence.

"Don't kill them!" Judy shrieked.

She tried to dive onto Cassie's back but slipped in her husband's blood, smacking face-first into the tile floor. Her skull *cracked* and Judy moaned, the lumps skittering away in fear from the wound forming on her face. Cassie's first instinct was to crouch down and check on her, but it proved to be a mistake; Judy snapped her teeth, the bloodied gnashers digging deep into Cassie's hand. Cassie screamed, yanking her hand away, but Judy held firm—until Cassie kicked her in the face. Judy yelped, and Cassie scrambled to her feet.

Cassie threw open the silverware drawer and grabbed the sharpest knife she could find.

"Don't do it," Judy moaned. There was fury in her voice, but it was fading as the blood poured over her face. Her fight was ending. "Don't. We can stay pretty, Cas. We can do it together."

"This is insane." Tears pricked Cassie's eyes. She didn't want to see her sister go like this. She looked down at the knife in her hand. "Please let me take them out. Let me save you."

"*Never!*" Judy thrashed on the floor with more strength than Cassie thought her sister had left. She rolled back and forth, her voice a low-pitched growl. "*Never. Never, never, neverneverneverneverr—*"

"Judy, please." Cassie's voice broke into a sob. She didn't want this. She never would have agreed to this if she knew how Judy would end up. "Please let me save you."

But Judy was gone, her defiant screams coming out into a wheeze. Cassie slid to the floor, unable to contain the overwhelming pain in her heart as she watched her sister fade into oblivion, leaving behind nothing but a husk for the bacteria to eat.

Cassie was not going to end up the same way.

Between the stream of tears, Cassie managed to hover the knife above one of her own lumps. She would end this. She would live.

Taking a deep breath, Cassie sliced the first parasite from her body.

LITTLE BOXES

LAUREN EVE

Keep quiet and breathe easy
  we'll take it from here
  stay still and remain calm
  we will keep you safe
  play dumb and act cute
  don't worry your pretty head
  stop overthinking it all
  the details don't affect you

... But they do, they *did*
they always will
placing us in little boxes
that we will always break through

will never contain our voices
won't ever stem the flow
of our opinions and independence
from the 'ideals' society condones...

keep your lessons and verses
out of my mouth
stay away from the people
that I choose to love

play up to the cameras
while we create a movement
stop pushing us backward
the future doesn't concern you.

BODILY

B. RAE GROSZ

There was nothing she could do but watch as they dug up her grave. It was the downside of being so new a ghost—she hadn't yet been separated from her body long enough to master the art of being incorporeal.

But being unseen meant no one knew she was there when he told them to bring her body back to him.

Being unheard made it all too easy to follow them to where she'd been buried.

She watched them dig up her grave. She waited until they had pulled her corpse from the coffin. Then, she slipped back into her flesh and bones. The upside to being so newly disembodied was that it was almost like she'd never left.

She waited a little longer, until the resurrectionists had delivered her to his door, until he had paid them for their service, until he thought he had her.

THE END

SARAH BELL

I'm drenched in sweat, my heart's pounding, and everything burns—my lungs, my legs, my eyes—yet I have to keep running. Through the haze caused by whatever the cops' chemical of choice is today, I follow the blur of black fabric that is the only one of my fellows still with me, and force myself to keep pace with them as racing footsteps thunder behind us.

Just one leg after another, again and again and again. When I feel myself flagging, when I want nothing more but to stop and catch my breath, I picture Mia Scott swinging from a noose. The first public execution in over a century, she was younger than I am now, not even out of her teens, but old enough to be tried and sentenced as an adult. They strung her up outside the Department of Justice and expected the crowds to cheer. Many did.

Me and Mom watched it on the television – some strange horrific compulsion as if we had to see for ourselves that it truly was happening. She stumbled on the scaffold, sobbing, and I nearly jumped out of my seat, as if I could reach through the screen and right her.

The rumor is her last words were, 'It was a miscarriage, I swear, please, please, don't do this!'

Some final part of me snapped that day. There's a string—pulled taunt—between that day and this one, leading to the hurried slap of my feet on the pavement, to the gun still warm in my pocket.

Though I've long known how my life might end, where my decisions might lead, I am not ready to share Mia Scott's fate. Not yet. So, I force myself to keep going, darting down alleyways, twisting and turning, never daring to look back, my breath harsh in my ears and my lungs.

"This way." My companion grabs my hand and pulls me down yet another alleyway with surprising force for someone of their slight stature. "I know a hiding spot." They wear a mask that hides their face as we all do, yet the glee in their voice means I can easily picture the grin hidden by the thick black polyester.

I pause, for just a second. It's not a part of the plan, but the plan is out the window now. The plan went out the window when the first shot rang out.

Mine was the third.

They pull me further into the warren of backstreets, and I follow as we scramble over fences and under collapsed telephone poles. The sound of pursuit slowly falls away. I only have a brief moment of relief before the sudden realisation that if this is a trap, I am already as good as caught.

"Here." They pry open a cellar door, half hidden by the weeds that push up through the cracked pavement. It slaps against the ground with a bang, and from the overflowing trash cans beside it, a stray cat startles and hisses at us. It's a void cat-like Familiar, fully black with amber eyes. I last saw Familiar howling with outrage inside his crate as Ma left. Looking back, it's almost like he knew the injustice of it all.

"It's okay, kitty." The words are a hoarse croak, forced out between my heavy pants for breath. They are the first words I've said since it happened. I take a step towards the cat, to try to calm it, to stroke it, but it hisses again and dashes down the alley.

"Are you done?" My companion watches me with wide eyes. The mask does nothing, ironically enough, to mask their expression.

Their disbelief is well-deserved. To be arrested, tortured, and killed because I stopped to stroke a cat would be a poor end indeed.

I nod and they scurry down the cellar stairs. "Make sure to close the door fully and lock it behind you or we're both dead."

There are no better options, so I do as they say. As the door falls into place, darkness envelops me. I reach out a hand to find the walls and instantly regret it. There's a cold, damp slime coating them and it sinks into my sweaty gloves to create some unholy concoction on my fingers.

It takes me some time to descend the stairs, groping at the gross walls, trying to be as quiet as possible. When my feet finally step onto a flat floor, I sigh with relief.

The slightest of chuckles from below me. "Sit. We could be here awhile."

"If the floor is anything like the walls, I think I'll stand." But my body begs me to sit. My breathing is still ragged, every part of me aches, and I'm shaking with the adrenaline still thrumming throughout my system.

"Oh, just sit!" It may be pitch black but I hear their eye roll.

"Fine." I sit, cold seeping across my bottom. I suppose I've been in worse places in the last four years, that barn out west coated with a selection of mystery animal—at least I hope it was animal—excrement springs to mind.

My companion has fallen mercifully silent, so I listen for any tell-tale signs of discovery from above, hands in my pocket clenching my gun, until...

"How old were you?"

It's the softest of murmurs, but I still start like they've shouted, and turn to stare in the general direction of their voice. We don't ask questions like that in The Rebellion. Hell, we even chose a name so bland it tells you nothing about us but the most basic of facts. Everything and everyone are anonymous, and there are rules to enforce this: code names and they/them pronouns only; everyone wears baggy dark clothes, and covers their hands and faces at all times; and no personal questions. The less you know about your fellows, the less you can betray them. Under torture is the part that goes unsaid, but understood nonetheless.

"We're not supposed to ask questions like that." It comes out tarter than I intended, like a scold. I've become Abigail Wright from middle school, our year's teacher's pet and snitch. The memory is as vivid as it is ludicrous. I haven't thought about Abigail in over a decade. She used to say she'd have eight kids by twenty-six, marry at eighteen and then birth one a year afterwards, always the little overachiever. Did she manage it? Does she regret it, if she did? Does she even have the time to regret it? Does she ever look at what's become of her life

and her body and her mind and wish the worst on
those who brain-washed her into believing this is
what she wanted?

I doubt she does. But maybe I am being unfair.
Maybe she has grown up since we were kids.
Certainly, I never would have thought my life was
heading here – to this cellar.

Maybe I should have. If I'm being honest, I
can follow that taunt string back past Mia Scott's
public hanging, back to the kid I was, who made a
poor choice and paid an unfair price.

It is my new mystery friend who pulls me from
my spiralling thoughts. They snort. "That's all you
have to say? It's not going to tell me who you are.
None of us are that unique."

"Then why ask?"

A beat of silence. "You shot that governor like it
was personal."

"Oh no, it wasn't personal." A lie. But they don't
need to know that.

"Okay." It's clear they don't believe me, which is
fair enough. "It was a good shot, though."

A warm pride spreads through me. It had been a
good shot. It took a hell of a lot of practice to get
that good. No one can say The Rebellion doesn't
teach its soldiers well.

"Are you from his state?" they continue, and just
like that my warmth disappears.

"I said it wasn't personal. I hate them all equally."
And I do. I hate every last one of the white men
that line the benches of that marble neo-classical

monstrosity, with their expensive suits and their smarmy voices and their overwhelming desire to inflict misery. If I have a little extra hate for Governor Wright, because I'm - as my companion here has so astutely figured out - from his state, because he signed the law that sealed my fate, well, they don't need to know that. Rules of anonymity.

"Hate them all equally, eh?" They repeat it disbelievingly. "Even better. You know how they hate equality." They laugh at their own terrible joke and I don't know what to say to that. Why are we even talking? This is just a distraction. I need to focus. We are still being hunted. I may have just become the most wanted criminal in the country. The realisation hits me with a dull thunk. I wait for whatever more reaction there is to come, but am greeted with nothing. Should I not be nervous? Worried? Scared?

When did I become so numb?

And does it matter? I'm a dead woman walking now. All that's left is the blaze of glory or the noose.

I will not let it be the noose.

I do not want people to cheer my execution. For Mom to have to watch that. And Ma, if she's even still alive...

I cut that idea short, shaking my head as if I can dislodge my thoughts, grateful for the dark. Thankfully, my new friend takes the hint and shuts up, and I focus once more on the sounds above, searching for anything out of the ordinary. But there's nothing but our shallow breathing and a few shuffling sounds from beside me.

"I was eleven."

It takes a few moments for the words to sink in, but when they do I jerk around, once more staring at a person I can't see. They haven't specified what exactly we are talking about, but I know. And we both know I know.

Eleven.

I'd heard horror stories, but it is another thing to hear someone so casually admit it.

"I'm sorry." What else is there to say, despite the meaninglessness of my apology? So much cruelty done to so many people and we're all sorry except for those who should be.

"Don't be." The smack of metal on flesh tells me they just hefted the pistol in their hands. They must have taken their gloves off. Careless. But what do the rules matter now?

I try to concentrate once more on the sounds above, but my mind keeps going back to the person besides me. Eleven years old and pregnant. All those changes, all that body horror and pain and trauma and shame, all the memories that I've suppressed for so long. At eleven. And then, as if that were not enough, there is the sobering reality of how an eleven-year-old gets pregnant.

But they are still here, fighting. Despite being perhaps the shortest and skinniest adult I've ever met.

Wait...

"How old are you now?" The question blurts from me.

"No ages, remember." They're teasing me. The damned kid – and I'm pretty horrifyingly certain they are in fact still a kid – is teasing me.

But then they speak again. "I joined The Rebellion at thirteen. I... I wanted to hurt them back."

And I know that want, deep in my soul. "Yes." The merest whisper. "Me too." It's a personal fact, no doubt, but they were right earlier. None of us are that unique. The Rebellion is full of people who want to hurt those who hurt us.

"Love that for us." It's an old meme – the sort of out-dated internet reference Mom would make, from back when she was young and jokes were merely nihilistic instead of literal gallows humor. Still, I can't shake the fact they are definitely still a teen. Maybe they also got it from their parents.

And I should not care about any of that. The many lessons our squadron leader, David, has drilled into us all cross my mind, followed by the much more solid thought that none of it matters anymore.

"Before or after The Execution?" I ask. Mia Scott's public hanging was far from the only one, but it was the first, and so it gets the capital letters.

"After. Just after." They are about fifteen then. "You?"

I suppose information has to go both ways. "Before."

"Before." A beat of silence. "So did you try to..."

They don't need to finish the sentence. It's not a word people say in public nowadays. And yet, here, in the privacy of this cellar, why the hell shouldn't I? "Have an abortion?" The words come out too fast, blurring together. "My mom looked up options." And I was lucky to have a mom willing to do that, but not surprised. I had two moms once, even if Ma is nothing more than a blurry face and a laughing voice in my memories. A woman who walked out the door whilst her cat howled his unhappiness to the world, and I watched the cat leave, because Ma's tears made me cry as well. Mom never forgave the dissolution of her marriage, nor the veiled threats that a child could not be brought up in a household of 'perverts'. She told me Ma left to keep us safe, because she loved us both too much to allow anything to happen to us. It was only as an adult I figured out how that could be true.

"Did she find any?"

The question brings me back to the present. I take a deep breath to steady myself. I will not cry in this cellar. That will not be how my story ends.

"Options, that is." They prompt when I don't answer.

"Mom managed to find a willing surgeon, but he charged $50,000 and not a cent less. His words, not mine."

They let out a low whistle.

"Exactly." We didn't have that kind of money. Not even close. James' father might have, but no way he would give it to me.

A loud bang from above makes me jump, then tense. I'd relaxed the hold on my gun as we talked, but I seize it again, cursing my wet and slimy gloves as it slides in my grip.

I listen, but there's nothing more but the quiet in-and-out of our regulated breathing.

"We didn't even consider it," they finally say into the quiet. "My mom figured it out in the end; I was far too scared to tell her. I thought she wouldn't believe me; would tell me I was going to Hell. All she did was hug me and tell me we would get through this together. But her and my dad didn't dare do anything but let me carry it. They tried to convince the doctors and the adoption staff to let them keep it. Raise it as my sibling. They were told in no uncertain terms they were lucky to keep me." They scoff, a lot of anger forced into such a short sound. "As if they had anything to do with..." They stop then and I do not probe. They will share if they want to.

No more words come from them.

"I tried to keep Ruby." The confession tumbles out of me. It's easier to talk here in the dark, with this stranger who might understand, knowing that soon enough I'll no longer be around for anyone to judge. "Not for any maternal reason. They sent a woman from that goddamned Family First adoption agency. She was right there at the hospital, waiting outside the room whilst I was still in labor. The same woman who spent my entire pregnancy telling me I wouldn't be a good mother, and that my best option was to allow my child to be raised in a good Christian home. Huh, all those damn pamphlets–"

"Oh God!" They shout. "Those pamphlets! Did you get the one with the stick figures?" Their tone turns mocking. "Like don't worry, it's okay, we have a PG-rated forced birth pamphlet just for the kids."

"What?"

"Oh, I take it you missed out on that particular delight?"

"I just got the usual ones talking about not dragging your baby down into your sin."

"Oh, charming! I didn't get those. Some advantages to being eleven, I suppose." Again, they say it far too casually. "Sorry, I interrupted. You were sharing..."

I try to remember what I was saying. "Right, yeah, so, those terrible pamphlets. And the doctors, so goddamn condescending. Everyone treating me like a silly kid, and perhaps I was, but it wasn't really my fault." And now I've started talking again, it's like I can't stop, all the things I'd tried so hard not to remember flooding back in. "I hadn't wanted any of it. I just wanted to see what it was like to sleep with a boy. I wanted to make James happy, because no matter how many times he said 'it's fine, we don't have to go any further' I could tell he was lying. And I loved him. I loved him so much. I thought we would get married one day."

"Did you want to get married?" Their scorn is obvious.

"Yes. No. I thought I did, but maybe that was just what I'd been told I should want. And I had other dreams: to finish school, go to college, become a vet – don't laugh, I've always loved animals and I was good at biology. But none of that mattered to them, so why should what they want matter to me?" The words are spilling from me, these regrets I've buried for over a decade. And the anger – the anger that's always simmering, that's driven so much of my actions these last four years, that made me pull the trigger earlier. That anger wants someone to know the damned truth. To hear it and understand.

"So what? You wanted to keep the kid because they wanted you to give it up." It sounds awful worded so bluntly. Selfish and bitter. But that's the stark truth of it.

"Something like that." My hands scratch against the floor, agitated. It's not like my gloves can get any dirtier. "They didn't let me, of course. Said they would have me and Mom arrested for child endangerment if I didn't give her up."

"Where is she now?"

"I don't know." Closed adoption. No information. And I never let my thoughts linger there long – a pointless endeavour. But it doesn't stop the familiar sting. The knowledge I have a daughter somewhere. Is she happy? Is there anything of me in her? She had James' hair, I remember that - thick, brown curls, even as a newborn. I ran a finger through them, even though they were still a little gunky. It was the only time I got to hold her.

"You could find out. I hear The Rebellion are planning to hack into the adoption records. Help us find our kids."

I shake my head and then realise they can't see it. I'm no one's mother. I never wanted to be a mother and I still don't. Maybe in a different life, in different times, when I could have made the decision for myself, but not in this one. My desire to keep Ruby was just a split-second selfish impulse to not be a good girl and do what they want of me.

But it would be nice to know that she's doing okay. That she's safe and loved. To know it as truth instead of just repeating it like a mantra.

James is a lawyer now - I certainly never would have seen that coming - and well-respected. If I could get him the information, could he find out that much? Surely, he wants to know, too. He punched a man from Family First - it cost his father a lot of money to cover that up - so I know he cared back then. But now? I don't know or understand the man he is now. Maybe he would go straight to the authorities.

And I'm getting ahead of myself. I have to still be alive for any of this to happen. Funny how easy it is to forget my death is probably imminent. Like the outside world has stopped existing – there's just this cellar and our shared histories.

"You're right," they agree, even though I haven't said anything out loud. "I'm no parent – I wouldn't even know where to begin. But I want to know he's safe – you know what some of those 'Good Christian Families' are like. And I'd maybe like to know him, for my parents to know him. They could be grandparents and I could be a big sibling like they wanted."

It's a wonderful notion and I want to disabuse them of it immediately. It's a fool's dream.

'You think it'll never happen." They are becoming eerily good at reading my silences.

I consider my words carefully, reminding myself they are young. "I think if The Rebellion may one day be able to do that, we are still a long way from that day."

"Huh, such a politician's answer."

I'm so offended I forget to be quiet. "You take that back!"

They burst into laughter.

"Shush!" My eyes dart upwards, as if I could see our potential assailants coming for us through the concrete above.

Their next words are sober, though. "David says this is the start of the end."

"David thinks making his code name a biblical reference will strike terror into our supposedly God-fearing opponents." It comes out sharper than I intended. This entire conversation is grating against my nerves. Maybe this is why we ask no personal questions, never mind potential torturers.

They snort at that again – the same casual amused sound – and somehow that soothes my anger. "I know David talks a lot of crap sometimes, but I do believe him on this. I have to." They sound so young on that last sentence. Fifteen, I remind myself.

"I know." Because it all has to be for something. Surely, this government will fall, like all tyrannical empires do eventually. This can't go on forever, but that day feels so far away, and I doubt I will live to see it.

"Do you think we'll die because of what happened today?" A quiet question with none of their earlier confidence.

"No." A lie. "No." I repeat it again, louder, as if that makes it any truer. We will have to leave this cellar eventually. The police and the national guard and the federal agents will all be swarming.

"You're a terrible liar." The scrap of their shoes on the floor and the rustle of fabric informs me they have stood up and started to walk away. Back towards the stairs, I assume, though my sense of direction is all twisted round in the dark.

"Where are you going?"

"I want to go down fighting."

"That's suicidal." But I stand, too, despite the protest of my numb legs and buttocks, and attempt to follow them. I nearly stumble straight back to the floor and by the time I've righted myself, I've lost track of where they are. "You should stay," I shout, desperation leeching into my voice. *Fifteen* is echoing in my head. They are too young to die. Too young to be here. Too young to have already survived all they have survived.

"No." They say it with such finality I can only nod—unseen—and argue no more.

I finally orient myself enough to join them where they have paused at the foot of the stairs.

We do not need to go up there. We could go back and sit down once more. Keep talking. Stay in this temporary refuge from all the cruelty and violence and fighting for just a little while longer.

But it will not change a damn thing.

"Sixteen," I answer their original question. The one that started all this in so many ways. "I was sixteen."

"Oh, positively ancient." But there's no bite behind their snarky remark. Then, they inhale deeply. "Ready to give them Hell?"

"We're the ones going to Hell, remember." But my hand crawls around my gun again until it slips. I remove my sodden gloves. And then the mask. The rules don't matter anymore. This is the end for us.

But maybe it is the start of the end, too. For Ma. For Mom. For Ruby. For my companion and their son, and for all the others out there like us. An end to all the grief and shame and horror. To the corruption and hypocrisy and cruelty in the name of a God who preached love.

The cold of the gun bites into my bare skin. Four years ago, I watched an execution and chose to fight, to believe the world could be better again, if we made it so.

I don't regret that choice.

TO BREAK THE WRISTS OF THE BUTTERFLY COLLECTOR

DANNY ST. VINCENT

you cannot so easily pin me down.

pin my palms nor pin my hips
to be crucified for your faith.
I am gossamer and fangs weaved into
the shape of rage.

try to touch the temple of my body
and I will leave your wrists in ruins.

there will be nothing left to collect but yourself.

you cannot so easily pin us down.

ACKNOW-
LEDGMENTS

This anthology wouldn't be possible without the financial help of so many people who backed the anthology's Kickstarter, including Andrew Joseph White, Barbara and Gordon Scott, Marissa (backer 69), Nico Hardiman, H.E. Edgmon, Robin Fisher, Joshua Leake, Christopher Wade, Carl Moyer, Jim Bertolini, Charlie Woodchipper, Han, Kimberley Hellem, Evelyn Silver, Neyla Downs, C.M. Rosens, Josie Angel, Nouh Bdee, Jeannie, Sam Scala, Zophia Pryzby, Francesca V., Corrin T., Cathy Green, Roselyne Caron, Magpie, Kyra Matsuda, Dayle Dermatis, Faysalkadow, Brittany Gross, Virginia Walker, Anna T., C.B. Blanchard, Gabriel Komisar, Kimberly Bea, Madison Howell, Louise Willingham, Rhys Dickel, Liz Wells, Perry Brown, Faiza Susan, Sebastian, and Phantoms Siren.

Thank you, K.M. Enright for polishing up our stories and helping them grow. You're absolutely stellar and working with you has been such a pleasure.

A massive thank you to the fabulous Therese for creating the last-minute chapter headers, and the wonderful Yasemin for the wrap-around cover. You two are gems and I am forever grateful for your help.

Shout-out to the original **My Say in the Matter** group chat who helped get this project off the ground. I wouldn't have had the courage to push forward with this if it weren't for Freydís Moon, Therese, scarecraux, Alta L. Turner, Scarlet Winters, and Victoria Weyland, amongst others already mentioned and who are in this anthology.

S.W. wanted to mention Annika Barranti Klein and David R. Slayton.

ABOUT THE AUTHORS

Alanna Felton (she/her) is a writer, feminist, and hopeless nerd. She recently graduated from Florida State University, where she spent her time writing a collection of feminist fairytales and protesting anti-abortion bills. You can find her book reviews in Shelf Awareness.

Stephanie Parent is an author of dark fiction and poetry. Her debut horror novel, *The Briars*, is forthcoming from Cemetery Gates Media in May 2023. Follow her on Twitter at @SC_Parent.

Morgan Daimler is the author of a variety of nonfiction books focused on fairies and Irish mythology as well as fiction based in Celtic mythology including the urban fantasy series *Between the Worlds* and the fantasy novel *Into Shadow*. They have also written a series of short story queer retellings of fairy ballads; their fiction usually features disabled characters, queer characters, polyamory, or some combination thereof with a strong focus on fantasy elements. They can be found on social media at https://twitter.com/MorganDaimler or https://www.facebook.com/Morgandaimler

Ezra Arndt (they/them/theirs) and they write queer gothic and grimdark fiction and poetry. They are a part-time author, part-time indie anthology curator/editor, and a full-time vampire enthusiast currently dwelling in Chicago, IL, USA. When not writing, they can be found reading, painting their story characters, and drinking obscene amounts of caffeine. They can be located at arndtezra.wordpress.com.

Sarah Grace Tuttle (they/she) is an author and poet living in Massachusetts with their partner and many plants. Their children's book *Hidden City: Poems of Urban Wildlife* was a 2018 Best Books for Kids according to the New York Public Library, and received a 2018 Eureka! Gold Medal from the California Reading Association. You can visit them online at www.sarahgracetuttle.com.

Alice Scott (she/they) is a queer author and indie bookseller who may or may not be a ferret turned human by a kiss from a prince. She has a BFA in creative writing from George Mason University and is the author of a number of short stories including SPITE or More Human in the

Grave. Follow them on Twitter @Allyscottauthor
for more.

Sam Amenn is an aro-ace, agender writer
who enjoys writing about angry queer
anthropomorphic crocodiles, demons, and giant
scorpions. When they're not writing, they're caring
for their spoiled dog, Queen Lola the Great, and
discussing asymmetrical warfare and colonialism
on their podcast: the Art of Asymmetrical Warfare.
To learn more about their writing, including
their upcoming book, Kingsley, follow them on
Instagram and Twitter (for however long it lasts)
@pepperdaphoenix and check out their website
https://pepper-writes.com/

Ceilidh Newbury (she/they) is an Australian
speculative fiction writer living on Tommeginne
land in lutruwita (Tasmania). She is a fierce
advocate for and creator of safe queer spaces,
especially for young people. They enjoy big
mugs of tea, singing to their cats, and can
be found screaming about books on Twitter:
@ceilidh_newbury.

S.W. Sondheimer is a Jewish, pansexual gore
spirit with chronic migraines and long Covid that
interfere with a great many things but not her
healthy book and Japanese stationery obsessions.
Her fiction credits include: "Punching Muses"
in *Three Time Travelers Walk Into...*, "Apocalypse

How?," in *Women in Horror 2016*, and "Memento Mori" in *Unlocking the Magic* (a fantasy anthology focused on mental health). Nonfiction credits include: "Hate Expectations: Politics and Gender Roles in the Expanse" and "The Long Dark Night of the Hat: The Metaphysical Fate of Detective Josephus Miller and His Headwear," both in the Expanse and Philosophy as well as a piece on the neurological connection between music and the writer's creative process in issue 10 of *Fantasy Art and Studies*. Her creative process is *Haikyu!!'s* Tanaka and Tsukishima in a hamster ball. A random generator once declared her genre "cactus garbage" and she stands by that. In her spare time, she is an amateur frog.

Marie Malo obtained an undergraduate degree in psychology and a diploma in Child and Youth Work in her Canadian hometown, before moving to the United States. She currently resides in the Midwest. She is working on her first novel, *Too Tangled to Move*.

Valerie Moore is a goth punk butterfly finally breaking out of her chrysalis. She enjoys writing poetry and experimental personal essays. When she isn't writing, she's active in her local pro-abortion and pro-immigrant organizations.

Paige N. Regan is a bisexual dark science fiction and fantasy writer with a penchant for chaos and cats. When she isn't caught writing in the middle of the night like a goblin, Paige enjoys streaming anime with her husband, playing cozy video games, and tending to the whims of her precious child (read: cat), Maple. You can follow her writing journey through Twitter, Instagram, Tumblr, and TikTok @pnrwrites or on her website at https://www.pnregan.com/

Lauren Eve became a poet by accident through late-night posts and is currently writing her debut novel. She recently released her independent debut collection, *A Graceless and Flourishing Heart.* Eve is an avid reader and reviewer of all genres but has a soft spot for Sapphic romances and YA thrillers. When her world isn't focused on books she can be found crafting or living out of a suitcase.

B. Rae Grosz (she/her) is an arospec, Pittsburgh-born writer, with a penchant for ghost stories, fairy tales, and folklore. Her work is often inspired by her struggles with ADHD, anxiety, and depression. Her free time is mostly devoted to entertaining her Border Collie. You can find her on Twitter @braegrosz and her TweetFic account @anotherStorying, or check out her website: https://braegrosz.com.

Sarah Bell is a queer indie author from Leeds, England. She has always enjoyed reading and writing since she was a child, and loves the chance to lose herself in other worlds and times. Outside of fiction, her interests include history and language. Her debut novel, *The Murder Next Door*, was released in June 2021.

Danny St. Vincent has always had a passion for creating and being a little bit of a horror, though he has an equal passion for dismantling manmade ones. When he's not lurking in the woods, he is painting and writing tales of the supernatural and the strange. A current project is a queer retelling of Swan Lake that explores themes that resonate with this anthology.

Made in the USA
Coppell, TX
14 February 2023

12768348R00134